THE RIGHT ANGLE CLUB

Annual Report 2011

Copyright 2011

Printed by Ross & Perry, Inc., 2011

© Ross & Perry, Inc., 2011 on new material. All Rights reserved.

Printed in the United States of America

Ross & Perry, Inc. Publishers
3 South Haddon Avenue, Suite 4
Haddonfield, N.J. 08033
Telephone (856) 427-6135
Facsimile (856) 427-6136
Visit us at www.rossperry.com
http://www.rossperry.com

ISBN: 978-1-932109-42-9

Book Cover designed by Just Ink

RIGHT ANGLE CLUB 2011

> As long as there is anything to say about Philadelphia,
> the Right Angle Club will search it out and say it.

My fellow Right Angle Club Members:

The 2011 Annual Report offers me the opportunity to thank my fellow Board of Control members and to report to the membership at large on the "State of the Club" in our Eighty Ninth (89th) Year.

The state of our Club is Excellent! The 2011 years saw an expansion of the modernization efforts begun in 2010 under our past President, Joseph A. Martinez, Jr. Beginning with the establishment of Affiliate Membership to stabilize and grow our membership and internet website development in 2010, our Club started with the 2011 President's Dinner to use web based event invitation and management program for Club Special Events. The web based system allowed members to register on-line without the need of mailing paper reservation to our Special Events Chairman, Mel Buckman.

Our Eighty Ninth year also marked the start of our "Friday Evening Buffet's at the Racquet Club of Philadelphia." The six evening buffets were designed to allow members to bring their wives, significant others or guests, to what is essentially the exact same social program as our members only Friday luncheons, also at the Racquet Club of Philadelphia. The Evening buffets were well received and attended. I suspect that our President-elect, John Fulton, will continue the program in 2012 but at a slightly reduced number.

There were some growing pains in 2011 that caused the cancellation of our traditional "Spring Fling." Due to uncertainty in our financial status, our long serving Treasurer, Rod Rothermel, advised the Board of Controls, that the Club was operating in a deficit [sounds familiar] and the Board voted to cancel the "Spring Fling." The Treasurer's report also resulted in several changes in the Club's traditional way of doing business.

First, a permanent Finance Committee was established to oversee the Club's financial activities. The Finance Committee is made up of the immediate past President as Chairman, [Joe Martinez 2011], member: 1st Vice President- Special Events Chairman, [Mel Buckman] and a member appointed by the President, [Jerry Leon 2011]. I want to point out and give a special thanks to the members of the Finance Committee for an excellent job and numerous hours of hard work given in service to the Club. Well done all!

Second, as it was discovered by the Finance Committee, the Board of Controls itself was unknowingly contributing to a chronic expenditure deficit due to the ten annual Tuesday Board of Control meeting held at the Racquet Club, despite an annual payment "to be Club" by all Board members. Starting in 2011, Board of Control meeting are now scheduled just before a regular scheduled Friday luncheon at a saving of several thousand dollars annually to the Club. Not surprisingly, the Board of Control meetings have now lost the traditional social and comradeship of the past. No small loss but a necessary one.

Third, the Finance Committee has implemented a 21st Century "Quicken" financial computer program to insure that uncertainty of the Club's financial status is no longer an issue in the future. The computer program will allow for a greater degree of fiscal control and budgeting. It is expected that on-line credit card payments for special events and ultimately Club dues will be offered in the near future. With acknowledgement to the extraordinary efforts of Special Events Chairman, Mel Buckman, the success of the Financial Committee was demonstrated by the our 2011 "Spring Fling" coming in under budget.

With our fiscal house in order, the Board of Control, under the leadership of our 1st Vice President, John Fulton, addressed the existential thread to the Club future, due to declining membership. In fact, in one month in 2010, the Club lost ten(10%) of its membership due to deaths or resignations. I can report to the Club that the negative trend has been reversed but we are not out of the woods. The "Member/guest Social" has been a proven success in attracting new members particularly 'Affiliate Members' that now number approximately ten (10)members. The Board of Control has capped the number of 'Affiliate Members' at any one time at 12 to protect the social tradition and integrity of the Club. The good news is that the 'Affiliate' Membership program has worked as planned with two 'Affiliate Members,' Dan Sossaman, Jr. and Steve Bennett, after experiencing Club activities, up graded their membership to 'Regular Full Member' in 2011. The Right Angle Club's membership is insure in the future of the Club by recruiting new members.

In 2011 the Board of Control turned its attention to the issue of membership retention through the use of the Club's first ever, Membership Survey. Special thanks are due to past Club President, Ted Burkett and Board member, Peter Alois, for design of the survey questions. The goal of the survey was very simple. The Board wanted to give all the Club membership the opportunity to give their opinion on the Club's programs and activities. Another surprise to this writer, almost eighty (80%) percent of the Club membership responded to the survey. The Results, which were forwarded to the membership, clearly show that the Club is headed in the "Right" direction. Membership satisfaction was extremely positive. No major changes in the Club's programs or activities are needed according to the 2011 Club survey.

No Right Angle Club job, and I mean job, is more difficult or nerve-racking [while waiting for the speaker to actually arrive] then 3rd Vice President-Speaker Chairman. A very special thank you and acknowledgment to our 2011 Club Speaker Chairman, Jerry Leon. Only a past Speaker Chairman can understand the hours of effort that go into securing some 35 to 40 speakers for the Club's weekly programs. Jerry had on advantage over most Speaker Chairman, he could stand up and just tell you the incredible events he experience in his life. Like flying jet aircraft in the Korean War with Hall of Fame great, Ted William and entertainer great, Ed McMann or being the infamous Lee Harvey Oswald's, Commanding Officer in Japan. Jerry's talks keep those lucky enough to attend on the edge of their seats. Great job Jerry! Simper Fidelis!

Our 2011 Club Special Events under the leadership of Mel Buckman, were the traditional activities of the Club with the "Fall Fling" at the Corinthian Yacht Club, the historic First Baptist Church of Philadelphia and the Christmas Party at La Viola West. Each event was an outstanding success as expected of the Right Angle Club. Well done Mel.

The great ship, 'RAC Board of Control,' does not sail by itself. I would like to thank our other officers, 4th Vice President, Jack Foltz, our raffle master; Treasurer, Rod Rothermel, paymaster; Archivist David McComack, ship's stories; Corresponding Secretary, Neale Bringhurst, signal master; Recording Secretary, David Richard, ship's logbook; Peter Alois, able body rower; Bill Hill, able body rower; Dan Sosseman, Sr., so so rower, [just kidding]. Well done, one and all!

Special thanks are also the Order of the Day for Jack Nixon and Buck Scott of our 2011 Club Nomination Committee and Chic Kelly, our Club Captain. Well done!

In 2011 the Board of Control was pleased to announce they had secured Reciprocal Club privileges at the Racquet Club of Philadelphia [RCP] for all members that include: 1) lunch in RCP lunchroom; 2) service at the Main [Players Lounge] Bar; 3) booking overnight room; 4) booking private parties; 5) Barbershop Privileges; 6) Happy Hours in Reading Room (May to September); 7) Wednesday nights buffers (September to May). Members merely have to identify themselves as Right Angle Club members and pay with a credit card. Right Angle Club members do not have charging privileges.

It is only fitting that I conclude this "State of the Club" report to our membership with some comments on 2012, the start of the Ninetieth (90th) year of the Right Angle Club. The 2012 President's Dinner at the Philadelphia Club will see the instillation of President, John Fulton. I can say without any doubt, that John will be overseeing the continuing modernization efforts begun in 2010 under our past President, John A. Martinez, Jr. The Club will continue to develop internet based events management, a first rate 21st Century web site with a current membership directory accessible only to Club members and on-line payment for special events and dues. John will be helped by the Club's first professional Webmaster, one of our own, Dan Sossaman, Jr. [or Younger...your call]. Why? To make life easier, a little less aggravating and allowing us, one and all, more time to "pursue happiness."

God speed, John J. White, past President.

Navigation Signals for Philadelphia Reflections

The particular browser program on a user's computer can sometimes make a big difference in its **screen display**. In the early days of the Internet, signals sort of like Morse Code were fired down the wire, one at a time but very fast. It was up to the receiving user to employ a browser program to turn on the little lights on the screen (pixels) in sequence, side to side, and up and down. To the naked eye, this organ concert appears like a movie screen. More modern machines moved on from this approach, but all computers still require browser programs for display purposes, and there are a dozen or so browser brands. New variations of each browser appear every few months, so there can be programs that just don't work with some of them. If you find you have a display problem, just change browsers and try again. **Browsers** are mostly free. However, notebook computers differ so radically from the rest that programs must be written or re- written for them to display anything. When *Philadelphia Reflections* is ready to display on notebooks, we will change this discussion. Portable telephones with computer features (iPhone, etc) are already converted; about half of *Philadelphia Reflections* visitors now use them. We must warn you however, that you can do more with a full-size machine that is half as expensive. The difference between a desktop, which can sometimes have a screen 30 inches across, and a handheld telephone with a 2-inch screen, puts a strain on technology and eyesight; the use of portable battery power creates another limitation. The following remarks are directed to users who have a desktop computer or a laptop. The other kinds of computer variants have their own systems which we will address elsewhere.

Philadelphia Reflections, like most desktop programs, has a home base or **front page**. By looking among the "options" or "preferences" of your browser, you will undoubtedly find provision has been made to display some particular front page every time you start the machine; you can arrange to have this program be your permanent starting point. More likely, you would want to look within the URL box and find the name of this program, preceded by a little Liberty Bell. That's called a **Favicon**. If you hold the left-hand mouse button down while you drag the URL by its favicon, you can deposit it on your desktop screen. There, it is unobtrusive, and

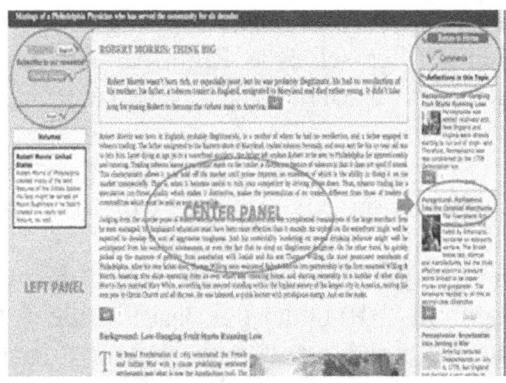

Philadelphia-Reflections

saves you the trouble of typing out WWW. Philadelphia-Reflections.com without making a typing mistake. By the way, notice that when text is either an unusual color or underlined, it often means it is linked to another file; double-click on it and the machine will switch to that other file. Go ahead and try it. You won't break anything, and at worst you will have to navigate back to this point in order to keep reading about navigation. You can also use the "Bookmark" feature of the browser in order to save the name of a particular program, or even a list of "Favorites". When they teach computer use in school, all of these features will probably be on the final exam and everyone will hate them, but at least so far, they are a big convenience used by surprisingly few people. Do yourself a big favor and make a note to learn at least one of them today. Life will become permanently easier for you. Guaranteed.

An overview of the front page of Philadelphia Reflections will illustrate that a page (which may be so big it runs off the bottom of the page) is organized into **three vertical columns, with a banner across the top**, and a collection of navigation icons (buttons) at the bottom. Then, satisfy yourself that the big center panel is a chain of five essays which change every ten minutes. At one time, a new page would appear without warning every ten minutes, but some people objected, so it now changes every time the user starts a new front page. There are usually five essays linked together in each refresh session, selected at random, and therefore devoted to almost any old topic. The original intention was to spread a wide variety of enticing subjects before a Philadelphia fan, just to show off what we've got. As things work out, five essays every ten minutes is enough for entertainment. If you have a specific interest, we have other ways of finding it for you.

For example, there is a little green box labeled **"Search"**, to be found in the far upper left-hand corner of the screen, just below the banner headline telling everyone how long I practiced Medicine in this city. Try typing in a likely topic, like "Art" or "Music" or "Revolutionary War". The machine will then search through every title looking for a match, and then display a few. If you double-click on the title of one, the machine will take you there and you can start reading. The search function is capable of indexing every word on the website, but there was not much interest, and it slowed things down. Some of the more modern browsers will retain a bread-crumb trail of where you have been, each step occupying a tab along the top of the browser's screen. If you are lucky, the browser you use will navigate you back to any stop along the way, just by clicking it. If you are planning to do some serious research or composition, taking the trouble to master this technique can greatly improve productivity. If not, you will probably find the browser manufacturer has modified it enough to require a new learning experience. Like *Philadelphia Reflections* there is a great deal of power hidden in the corners of most browsers. You never know when it will prove useful, like the dials on the dashboard of your car.

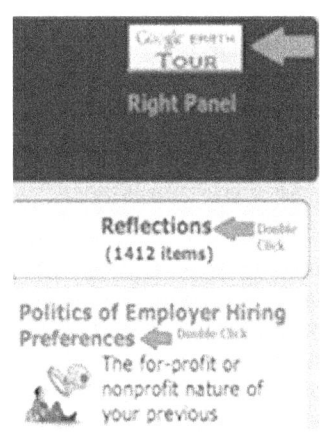

Beneath the Search box is a blue bar to double-click if you want to **subscribe to our weekly newsletter**. There are several advantages to doing so. One essay a week may be enough for a casual reader, and the email which delivers it contains a link to the website, which is still another way to get here if you can't remember the name, or have dyslexia and can't spell it. Finally, intruders have stolen some part of my name or the site at least a dozen times, and it may become necessary to change the name or the address to flee from this. If it comes to that, it would be handy to have a way of notifying loyal readers about the new location. By the way, if you suspect identity theft, or phishing, or something else of that nature, the agency to call is the U.S. Secret Service. Not the FBI or the local police, or the CIA or your congressman. The Secret Service, an essay about which is part of this website.

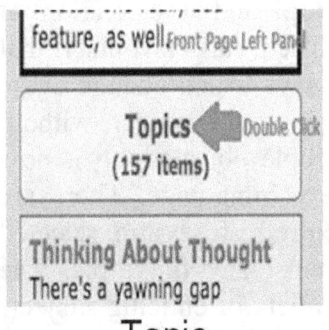

Topic

Moving ahead, let's look at these same essays grouped as **Topics**. That reduces the current number to about 150, and many of them are incomplete, under construction. Go to the front-page box called Topics and double-click it. The link will then display boxes with short abstracts, and double-clicking one of them will display from three to seventy essays (blogs) devoted to that topic. That at least will group the same subject together, and some of these topics have been organized in order, creating a narrative. At the top of the right-hand column is a button which will allow you to print the topic, and depending on your machine, possibly create a PDF file, modify the type font and margins. Lower on in the right hand column are little abstracts of each blog in the topic, and double-clicking on the bold-faced title will cause the machine to **go to an individual blog**, possibly for printing. Many of these blogs have a **geo-tag**, and **display a map of the region** around it, peppered with tabs leading to other blogs about locations within the map area.

You can **go back to the front page** by double-clicking the yellow stripe at the bottom of the Home box, and if you do you will see that about a **hundred most recent blogs** are listed down the right-hand column. It's been surprising to me how often readers want to look at what has been written recently. After all, this is mainly a compilation of material from three centuries of history. But from time to time there is a commentary on something recent, so here you are.

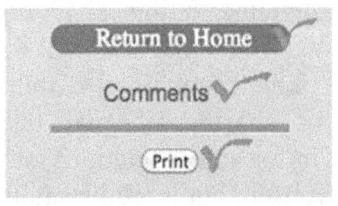

Home-Box

http://www.philadelphia-reflections.com/blog/2172.htm

Navigation Signals for Deeper Levels

L et's call the front page "Level One". On it are several "icons" for drilling down to "Layer Two." An icon is a small portion of the screen which has been **"activated"**, a condition which can be identified from the way the cursor changes to another picture when you roll the cursor over that point, and changes back to the more familiar arrowhead when you slide off the active area. Usually, the icon indicating "active area" is a cartoon of a hand with a pointing finger. If you click or double-click on the active area, the program

Comments

switches to the underlying program on the second layer. Quite often, the screens on deeper levels also have active areas, allowing you to "drill down" sequentially to an unlimited number of deeper levels. All of this makes it hard to discuss the navigation in words, although it's easy enough to display a picture of it. Our program often has three or four layers, but sometimes only two. The first discussion of Navigation Signals discusses the top two layers, and this second discussion explains the deeper layers collectively. We assume you intuitively get the general idea without the tedium of dragging you through engineering drawings. If you let us know in the "Comments" what remains unclear, we will try to clarify the labels. For the most part, navigation difficulties grow out of not realizing a potential exists, rather than difficulty finding it. For that reason, we suggest you cruise around the screen and take a look at anything which signals it is active.

But let us know; we'll try to clarify the directions until they are crystal clear.

The first deep-level discussion is about **printing**. Almost all full-size computers attach to a printer, and a lot of people prefer to use that to print out these articles rather than read them from the monitor screen. Some people have trouble with their eyesight; most printers will magnify ("zoom") the image if instructed to. For extreme cases, we are engaged in a project of creating "podcast" oral readings, but that is far from complete. We place these readings on iTunes, where you can adjust the volume or repeat the performance. The little blue bar in the upper left corner of most pages will get you into the table of contents of this system. We are also beginning to embellish it with "Soundslides", which play the voice in the background while displaying a slide show of the images. It's also possible to create little videos, with sound and in color, and place them on U-Tube, but that's a lot of work and will be slow 'acoming.

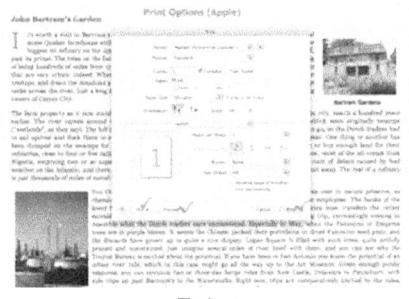

Print

For now, concentrate on plain old printing. Almost all browsers have a "print" command within the FILE drop-down on the command strip. However, it's usually pretty crude and prints everything on the monitor. We supply you with a "print" button on most pages, which discards much of the browser material, displaying only the content window. Specifically, it creates a PDF image, and the free Adobe reader will then print it out on paper all formatted nice, creating photos of the content to store as if they were a collection of photographs. Adobe is busily adding features, and you can often add comments to a PDF page, display them as a slide show, or print them on your printer as a book. All of this will depend on the kind of browser, print program, and printer you have, and whether your computer is compatible with them. However, you can now buy a pretty fancy printer for less than a hundred dollars, so why not. Be sure to get one that can print on both sides of the paper ("duplex"), and prints with a laser beam if you plan to do a lot of printing. Ink cartridges for printing in full color are expensive, black-and-white is usually adequate.

Turning to another deep-level function, you can **search** this whole program, in a way very similar to the way you can search the whole internet. Type the word in the box, and then click on the word "search". At the moment, it only searches the titles of the volumes, topics and reflections, although the capability exists to index every word of the site. That may be of some use to scholars, but for most readers it makes the results-list too long. It might not be a bad idea to index the captions below the images; let us know what you think.

It's a pesky thing to maintain a table of contents to a website which is constantly enlarging. The search function may be an adequate substitute for most users. However, we provide you with the titles and abstracts, and offer to **sort** these boxes into several different sequences. If you want the most recent products, you probably want the sequence labeled "Most Recently added". The reverse chronological sort is more or less available as "Numerical". For the most part, however, the demand will be for alphabetical or reverse-alphabetical sequence. Once you find what you

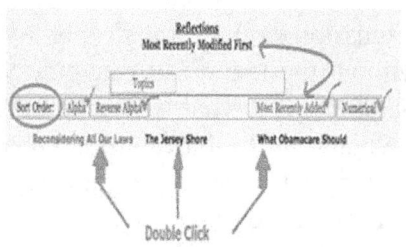

Most Recently Added

want, double-clicking on the bold-face titles within each box will cause that particular item to be displayed, and its icons will be activated as well, allowing you to drill still deeper.

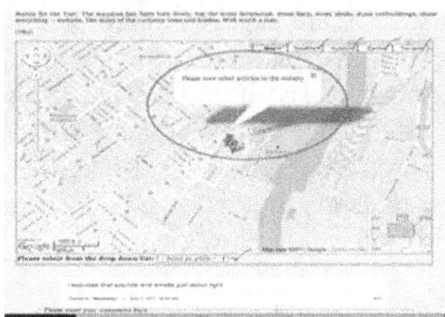

Google Map

The **map** function is provided by Google, who keeps adding features. Be sure to try out each one of the Map-Satellite-Hybrid-Earth-Terrain buttons on a map you are familiar with; you may be amazed at the potential that suggests itself. These maps are generated whenever a blog has some sort of geographical feature. We can give you Independence Hall but Taxation without Representation is a little hard to locate geographically. Once some physical point is established, however, your machine can tell how big the map is, and look up whether any other blogs are within its boundaries. Therefore, the pin in the center gives you this location, and the red flags direct you to blogs which are geographically nearby. That's designed to help tourists who are walking or driving around the site. Yes, you can move the map around to conduct your own searches.

Comments are something we wish more users would use. It's very useful to have a thousand eyeballs looking for mis-spellings and factual errors; we promise to correct them promptly. When *Philadelphia Reflections* was started in 2003, we thought it might provoke more historical commentary or even challenge than it has. Perhaps it was a mistake not to insist that commenters list their email address, but we decided not to invade your privacy. If you want a reply, therefore, we have to ask you to send us an email directly, using the "Contact Us" button at the very bottom of almost every page.

http://www.philadelphia-reflections.com/blog/2175.htm

Gum

The ancient Greeks and Romans are said to have enjoyed a sort of chewing gum. The ingredients are uncertain but unlikely to have been chicle, the sap of a variant rubber tree, which was taken up by the Mayans in the First century. The vision thus ensues that Mexican soldiers might well have been chomping when they set out to conquer Texas and devastate the Alamo. Conceivably Santa Ana himself was popping bubbles when Sam Houston found him crawling through the tall grass when he should have been dying like a man.

What is not so fanciful is that Santa Ana did go into exile in the United States, seeking refuge on Staten Island. Taking along a large supply of chicle, he was hoping to find a way to change it into rubber and thus restore his fortunes. His New York landlord, a photographer named Adams, struggled unsuccessfully for months to change the gum into rubber, but eventually switched over to chewing gum of chicle. This Mexican rubber variant is chewy only

Gum Bubble

within a narrow temperature range, getting brittle when cold, and sticky when hot. The outcome of this bizarre episode was the Adams brand of chewing gum, a dominant feature of our

General Santa Anna

culture until 1922 when William Wrigley, Jr. of Chicago added a mint flavor and made a great fortune selling the hope that minty taste would clean your teeth, sweeten your breath, and improve attractiveness to the opposite sex. Wrigley must have been a great businessman, since the Wrigley Building still dominates central Chicago, while everyone knows about Wrigley baseball field, and his descendants even run a private railroad through the Copper Canyon south of Tucson into Mexico. Wrigley's winter mansion sits on top of a small mountain outside of Phoenix, once affording a grand view of the surrounding desert for many miles. But subprime mortgages helped build up the desert; so at night there is now a sparkling view of the lights

of Phoenix suburbs, longingly gazing up at Wrigley's mountain fastness filled with pictures of relatives who got themselves great notoriety, mostly related to unfortunate escapades with love.

Well, whatever. By 1960 a cheaper synthetic chemical came to replace chicle in Chiclets without distressing the customers, and seemingly making it commercially practical to spread this central feature of American culture to Asia, Europe and beyond, with the notable exception of France which makes their cultural superiority a point of national pride. On further reflection, if they prefer vintage chicle to the present chemically improved synthetic, the French may have an important insight. Just look at our filthy sidewalks.

Gum on the sidewalk

Other cities may be more diligent in scrubbing their sidewalks, but at least in Philadelphia, the new synthetic chewing gum is leaving its mark. The realization gradually creeps up on you that sidewalks near popular corners of center city are spotted with round black spots, slightly larger than a silver dollar, but uniformly black. Just what the sidewalks around high schools look like, I tremble to consider. But those city corners where a sidewalk vendor parks his cart are particularly peppered, representing the disgusting habit of spitting the chew-gum on the sidewalk before eating the hot dog. The detritus is flattened out by someone's shoe, and the result is quite distinctive. As I was contemplating a particularly loathsome street corner, a passing Philadelphia *Grand Dame* shared her insight with me that the gum attracts dirt and gets black. I somehow doubt that because it is such a uniform blackness. It seems more likely that the trade secret chemical deteriorates in the sunlight, and being less sticky than the traditional goo, sticks to the sidewalk instead of the shoe which squashes it.

So think this over. Someone was recently chewing that stuff; would you kiss that person? If it's fresh enough, it might transmit the flu virus to your shoe; ye Gods, maybe the HIV virus, perish the thought. There's a great absence of evidence about the disease transmissibility of this unknown material. Maybe our congressmen should take a recess from blaming Wall Street for the decline of Greece and Portugal. And make chew-gum scoopers just as mandatory as pooper scoopers.

Footnote: A fellow member of the Right Angle Club recently revealed he had once worked for the Philadelphia Chewing Gum Company in Havertown, which was closed by new owners in 2003. While he didn't know anything about the ingredients of gum, he could report that this company used trainloads of old rubber tires for some purpose. On further checking, it is stated in the literature that at the present time, no chewing gum *doesn't* use rubber, so apparently Santa Ana's dream has finally come true in a round- about way.

http://www.philadelphia-reflections.com/blog/1837.htm

Mennonites: The Pennsylvania Swiss

Anabaptism grows from believing a baby is too young to understand baptism, so adults need to be re-baptized. The idea arose independently in Switzerland and Holland around 1525, and probably thousands of believers were unmercifully martyred for holding the belief. The Swiss adherents moved to the Rhineland Palatinate, and from there were among the first to accept William Penn's offer of religious freedom. They were the settlers of Germantown, but have mainly moved a few miles west to southern Montgomery County, where the confusion about Pennsylvania Dutchmen is further confounded by the fact that they were Swiss. Menno the Dutchman gave his name to the order, but they regard their true ethnic background as Swiss from the Zurich region. That, by the way, is not to be confused

On the wall of the
Mennonite Heritage Center

with Calvinism, which also comes from Switzerland, but from Geneva, not Zurich. The pacifism of the Mennonites made them mutually attractive with the Quakers, who came along fifty or so years later from the region around Manchester, England; each group seems to have adopted some of the features of the other.

Determined use of the German language has always held the Mennonites apart, however. From the start, it was necessary to be somewhat bilingual, using English for business conversation, and

German at home and in the church. The idea of using a foreign language is based on the hope of thus maintaining a sense of distinctiveness or even remoteness from non-believers without adopting the least hostility to them. It almost inevitably follows that the group has used its own schools, attached to their meeting houses. This sense of remoteness has persisted for almost four hundred years, surrounded by entirely different cultures. Starting only around

Franconia Mennonite Meetinghouse

1960, this attitude has gradually softened, and it is widely assumed that in another few decades they will come to resemble the people in their environment a great deal more than they do at present. If you want to know where to find them, Harleysville is a good place to start. As the tinge of Pennsylvania Dutch accent gradually fades, and fewer of them wear the old costumes, a curious remaining hallmark of their presence can be noticed: an avoidance of foundation planting around their houses. The Mennonites themselves seem to be entirely oblivious to this unintended distinctiveness, which is however quite apparent to non- Mennonite passers by. Those who work in the fields all day have little interest in digging around their houses for decoration; those who have moved away from farming have seemingly adopted the bush-less style as a natural way of arranging things. There's no particular reason to change it, and so, there's no particular reason to notice it.

http://www.philadelphia-reflections.com/blog/2038.htm

South Philadelphia: Ideal Intermodality Transportation Site

The Right Angle Club was recently visited by Troy Adams, representing the Greater Philadelphia affiliate of the regional Chamber of Commerce. Sustained by contributions from sixty local corporations, the Greater Philadelphia organization is a major storehouse of data useful for businesses, supported by a staff of analysts and computer experts. The purpose of this institution is to help businesses who are trying to decide whether or how to locate in the Philadelphia region. With such an organization behind him, Mr. Adams was able to show a number of slides displaying the demography, geography and statistics about our region, and his appearance is greatly appreciated. This is definitely the place to go if you have questions of that sort. It would

Troy Adams

probably also be a good place to go for opinions and gossip about the politics and inside baseball of the town, but the Chamber has a strict rule about avoiding any involvement in business moving from one district to another within the region, or hearsay that might lead to such internal friction.

One really important insight into the potential of our region concerns South Philadelphia. Historically, this was the place where the Schuylkill and Delaware Rivers met, and was once a very big swamp (wetland, nature sanctuary or whatever). Over time, the swamp became a trash and garbage landfill, and over still more time it became a big flat uninhabited area right next to a big city. But then an Interstate Highway (I95) was built on its circumference, and several rail lines, and an international airport, not to mention extensive port and shipping terminals for ocean transport. While it is true that a certain number of houses would have to be purchased and demolished to accomplish it, the potential exists for the construction of an intermodal interconnection which would be almost unique in the world.

South Philadelphia Ports

There would be plenty of land left over for industries related to freight forwarding and the like (the food distribution center is a good example of the general concept), and all of this would be within twenty minutes of the center of a major city. SEPTA already sends a passenger rail spur from the very heart of the city to the very center of the airport, and there is no reason it could not be extended to include ocean, bus, and distribution terminals. Whether this exactly fits with the extensive sports stadium complex in the area is unclear; but these entertainment features are doing no harm to the intermodal interchange idea in the meantime. Judging by the city government's willingness to tear these structures down every five or ten years, there should be no great resistance to moving them elsewhere if the need should arise.

http://www.philadelphia-reflections.com/blog/2060.htm

Net Neutrality and Vertical Integration

My fancy new cell phone has an annoying habit of ringing a bell every time an e- mail arrives, which is a little puzzling when it rings in the middle of the night. The email program displays time of arrival, so after a while I took the trouble to see who was emailing me at 4 AM. It seems to be spam, and other commercial programs, but it is also an occasional letter with a large attachment, which had been sent several hours earlier. At this, a light began to go on in my head.

Late Hour Calls

I had been told the internet measures the size of files, and puts big ones at the end of the queue. That seemed to explain the occasional delayed transmission of ultra-large emails at times of heavy internet traffic. And it brings up the issue of net neutrality. If the traffic in large files grows enough, it might eventually clog the wires and bring things to a halt. The internet providers would have to spend money to build additional capacity, and it only seems fair to charge the big users more for the costs they have created. That would seem a reasonable technological argument for allowing the networks to impose differential pricing, and for overturning the idea of net neutrality.

Comcast and NBC

Unfortunately, it might or might not be a sincere argument for resisting net neutrality, since there are major commercial issues at stake as well. For example, Comcast is trying to purchase NBC; its motives are clarified by remembering that a few years ago it tried to purchase Walt Disney. In both cases, a common carrier would be acquiring a "content provider", and thus acquiring a competitive advantage over competitive internet network providers who lack a captive source of content. A strong temptation would exist to slant the internet charges to the disadvantage of other competitors, thus providing a motive to get involved in insincere arguments about net neutrality. What we seem to have here is a familiar antitrust legal doctrine of "vertical integration". For years, vertical integration was prohibited, but the U.S. Supreme Court reversed that prohibition a few years ago, in the case of State Oil v. Kahn. Lewis van Dusen and I had been in the audience of the State Oil arguments, because of our interest in the implications of vertical integration for the medical profession (doctors versus hospitals, for example).

Although the example of Curtis Publishing was not introduced into the arguments of State Oil versus Kahn, it was much in my mind and might well have been used effectively to demonstrate the vulnerability of any corporation which attempts to become vertically integrated by purchasing its suppliers and/or distributors. Curtis Publishing, a few blocks from my office, had been a successful magazine publisher, so successful that it had enough profits to buy Canadian forests to use for paper pulp in its magazines. The outcome was the bankruptcy of the profitable magazine company when the paper pulp

Curtis Publishing

business fell on hard times. No antitrust action to prohibit vertical integration was necessary; the dismal fate of Curtis and similar integrators stood as an effective restraint on anyone else who was tempted to get into the vertical integration business. That may be a little hard to follow, and it took the Supreme Court many years to get to that point. But the fact remains that vertical integration is no longer illegal, because it is effectively restrained by recognition of its dangers.

So, if we are getting into the insincere argument business, it is time for someone to put his arm around the shoulders of Comcast. Let's whisper that avoidance of the net neutrality dispute is kindly advice, offered solely for Comcast's own good.

Comcast Center

And, having gone this far in poking into other people's business, there might be some value in giving some advice to the antitrust lawyers. This sort of case can take years, even decades, to evolve through the legal system. And while its resolution will be phrased in legal terms, I'm not so sure that's sincere, either. It takes me back to the IBM case, where one of the junior lawyers was courting one of my daughters. This young fellow sat for months in front of a microphone at a deposition, doing nothing but read documents into the record. Although he was handsomely paid, the lawyer finally got so sick of the boring futility of dictating a mountain of transcript no one would ever read, into a microphone in an empty room, that he quit. And in the opinion of observers on the courthouse steps, the case was finally determined by the Judge's decision that the patent infringement business was trivial compared with the fact that IBM was mass-producing the greatest innovation of the century.

That may or may not have been the case, but it raises the question of whether antitrust law is wisely based when it considers, not the welfare of competitors, but the strength and vitality of competition itself. What might thus be considered paramount, and perhaps occasionally is so, is the economic welfare of the nation.

http://www.philadelphia-reflections.com/blog/2054.htm

Do Computers Thrive on Lead Poisoning?

At a local outlet of a well-known chain of computer stores, the geek told me that small computer towers don't last as long as big-box desktops, perhaps only three years compared with the old five-year lifespan. And that's because they get hotter. Which is because they run faster than they used to, and also because a federal regulation prohibiting the use of lead in soldering joints makes the wiring wear out sooner. By the time he was done explaining things to me, I was ready to run out and join the local political Tea Party. Because I don't think it's very likely that toddler children will be eating my solder very soon, or even ever. And indeed, I have trouble imagining any children anywhere in the world ever nibbling on computer innards, even once. Maybe the concern is that the heat will vaporize the lead, and little children crawling on the floor will inhale lead vapor, getting lead poisoning that way. While that may be somewhat more plausible

Get the Lead Out

than eating computer parts, or eating vegetables grown in the neighborhood of trash disposal, or breathing the air full of lead fumes – it doesn't really seem very plausible at all.

It is generally reckoned that 835 million computers world-wide were manufactured in 2010. If they cost an average of $500 apiece, and lasted 40% less long than if they used lead solder, the world would end up buying 300 million additional computers per year, conservatively spending $1.5 billion more dollars a year to do so. Are the dangers of lead poisoning so threatening that such a cost is justified on a hypothetical basis? The people who do the soldering are possibly at somewhat greater risk, but you could buy a lot of masks and air purifiers for the extra cost for computers alone. Can this possibly be true?

Is it possible that the geek in the computer store is just selling warranty insurance, or more expensive computers when he passes on this news? Is it possible that the makers of fumes ventilators are promoting their products in this way? How about the plaintiff trial lawyers. Are they calculating that frenzied citizens will wander into jury duty and be concerned to punish the evil makers of computers with gigantic penalties, of which the lawyers will get 40%? Or the makers of cool computer boxes are competing indirectly with the evil makers of hot computer boxes?

This article ends with a comment section. Those who can offer references to the facts in this case, are urged to send them in. Something in this story doesn't stand the light of day, and perhaps a way can be found to shine a little light of day on the facts.

http://www.philadelphia-reflections.com/blog/2056.htm

Future Directions for Book Authoring

Here's some advice for new authors of books: *You can't write the first chapter until you have written the last chapter.* That is, you have to hit the reader between the eyes in the first chapter, draw him into the argument, making a pauseless transition from a general statement of the author's thesis into a relentless march of evidence toward the conclusion. This general design comes easier with practice and is therefore much harder for beginners to accomplish. But even experienced authors are usually unable to keep the overall design of their message constantly in mind, to be able to sit down and write the book straight through from beginning to end. It's true that Sir Walter Scott was said to turn over the last page of a book, and immediately begin writing the first page of the next one without getting up from his desk. But we aren't talking about pot-boilers, we're talking about serious books. That includes almost all non-fiction, and the great majority of serious fiction.

TRS-80/100

As a matter of fact, the description includes the majority of short articles as well; newspaper editorials would be a good example. Although the style of an editorial is to start with a generality, marshal a description of some recent events, and end up with a short summary, that isn't in fact how it is usually composed. The editorial writer starts with a one-liner, or call to action, organizes some recent events and some historical arguments as a reason to issue such a call, and then ends up by summarizing things in the first paragraph. Having mentally designed the editorial into such a three-step pattern, with experience a professional editorialist can sit down and write the editorial from beginning to end and, after a few touch-ups, it's ready for the printer. He really has gone through the organizational process which a book author needs to go through, but the article is short enough so that reconstruction is performed in his head. In a book, it is generally necessary to write out the chapters in a jumbled way, and later re-organize them. A new author with his first manuscript generally doesn't adequately appreciate the truth of this and has to be muscled by the editor, at least just a little bit. One of my editors summarized his job as follows: you tell every new author to take the first four chapters of his book, and throw them away,

That's cruel, of course, and is seldom accepted graciously. The brusqueness is justified by understanding that the fresh new author thinks he's all finished when he isn't. He's silently telling himself he means to tell that editor, "Don't you touch a single comma of it." In the old days, authors were rare and had to be coddled. Book publishers in the Eighteenth century purchased the manuscript in its entirety, either then losing money or making a huge fortune, but leaving the author with only his manuscript price. At that time, publishers called themselves booksellers. As things evolved, booksellers often had to support a starving author while the book was being written, offering an "advance" payment to be deducted from royalties paid after final sales to readers. Author royalties were about ten percent of sales. The royalty system persists today, but advance payments are uncommon and negotiated around the tax code effects. All of these payment evolutions reflect the underlying issue: good authors used to be rare, but now are frequent. Book publishers used to be wealthy, but now are rapidly going bankrupt and extinct. Authors of excellent books have a hard time finding someone to publish them. The advent of the personal computer around 1980 is what caused this.

In 1980 I published a book, writing it on my brand-new Radio Shack TRS-80, Mod I. The editor of the publishing house had never heard of such a notion, scoffed at it, and declared he would never touch such a thing as a computer. In 2010 there were more than 800 million personal computers manufactured and sold, and by this time almost no publisher will accept a manuscript without an accompanying magnetic disc to make revisions cheap and easy, and to shift the costs of key-entry from the publisher to the author. At first, manuscripts were shipped to India for key entry. Now, it is the diskette which is mailed or e-mailed to India, and the editor is often located in India. We are soon approaching a day when the keyboard and author remain at home, sending material to gigantic server computers in China, from which the editor anywhere in the world can retrieve the material and revise it, returning the material to the server computer where the author can comment on the revisions without moving from his desk. After that stage, looms the prospect of the reader paying a fee on his credit card to access the "book" directly from the server, and reading it at home. At that point maybe the book will have been completed, and maybe it will be revised some more. In a sense, a book will never be definitely finished, and allowing the public to read it will only be an episode within an unending process of revision. Newspapers, magazines and books are all struggling to find a way to cope with this unpredictable evolution. Like most revolutions, this one doesn't have a clear idea where it is going.

So let's reflect back on the central process of authoring. In addition to the old maxims of the trade, there is the Euclidian reality that you can't write the last chapter until you somehow write a first one. The original first chapter, the one the author struggled so hard to compose, is destined to be cast off and replaced by a new first one, one that succinctly announces what is about to be said. After that must come a new second chapter, which takes the reader from the initial disconcerting summary back to the origins of the problem now about to be clarified. Followed by a third chapter, probably one shifted forward from the assorted chapters of evidence back into prominence as the key piece of evidence which leads to other confirmatory pieces of evidence; after that marches the parade of confirmatory evidence, ending with one zinger of a conclusion.

Voltaire or some other cynic would probably comment that what has here been outlined is merely an elaborated process of what editorial writers do: start with the conclusion and find slanted facts to fit it. Some may indeed do that. But there is some hope that the inevitable impact of technology on authorship can bring us to a system where many authors will assemble the facts, and only then derive a conclusion from them. If politicians would only adopt that system, maybe we could hope for a perfect world.

http://www.philadelphia-reflections.com/blog/2062.htm

Recalling the Names of Acquaintances

As age creeps up on us, just about everyone has a little trouble recalling the name of old acquaintances, particularly if they come upon us unexpectedly. Reactions to this affliction vary tremendously, with some folks concluding that Alzheimer's Disease is surely here already, so they run away and hide. Other seniors are more self-confident, and unashamedly go ahead with little strategies to cope with this problem. When you sort things out, you tend to find that shy and retiring people withdraw from social contacts because of self-consciousness, while bluff, bold extroverts plunge ahead with strategies they have devised to cope with matters. Neither one of them can remember a lot of names.

Speaker on a Soapbox

The extroverts are usually very happy to share their secrets; a whole social group can be transformed by one loud, happy, unashamed coper, sharing his techniques.

Times Square

The late Doctor Francis C. Wood, formerly Professor of Medicine at the University of Pennsylvania after whom a number of professorships, institutes and lectures are named, once made a little speech at a reception held at the College of Physicians of Philadelphia. "When you see somebody at a party whose name you ought to recall but can't, just stride right up to him with your hand held out. Just say your name like a gentleman, like 'Fran Wood,'" and he will invariably grab your hand gratefully and tell you his name, like 'Jim Jones, Fran. How are you?' After that, you'll get along just fine."

This isn't a medical matter at all. It's a matter of self-confidence and learned techniques. Dick Maas, who is a resident of the Beaumont CCRC in Bryn Mawr PA, was recently proud to describe his own technique in the *Beaumont News* as follows:

Handshake

"Let's start with the obvious conclusion that one can't remember something one didn't hear in the first place.

Introductions often are given in a social situation, which usually means one is surrounded by loud noise. Furthermore, the person doing the introduction may have a soft voice or poor diction. There's hope, however. One can employ a little trick that's socially correct and psychologically useful: Shake hands with your new acquaintance! Hang on until you hear the name clearly and correctly. If necessary, hang on and say, 'I didn't get your name. Would you please repeat it?' Even ask for a spelling if need be. Don't release the hand until you've heard it correctly and repeated it back."

It isn't always necessary to use a name or shake hands. In Haddonfield where I live, the custom grew up years ago that everybody says, "Hello" or "Good Morning" (Good Morning preferred) to everybody one meets on the street – before lunch. There's no hesitation about it, that other person is going to say "Good Morning," so you might as well get ready for it. Of course, it's true that some people don't know what to do with themselves, and retreat back into their shells, awkwardly trying to pass you by without acknowledging your greeting. You can either shrug your shoulders and assume that repetition will gradually bring that newcomer around in a few days or weeks, or else you can refuse to let them do that to you. Step in his way and say it louder. To get away with this you have to be prepared to say something about the weather or your dog or the morning news, which is a pleasant way of saying you weren't belligerent about it, just showing them the way things are done in Haddonfield. Pass yourself off as uncontrollably extroverted. And be sure to smile. This sort of custom is a matter of population density. Up in Alaska a trapper who passed within a mile of another trapper's cabin without saying, "Howdy" was inviting a knife fight about the insult. In New York's Times Square, by contrast, a pedestrian is within walking distance of two hundred thousand people; greeting everybody is an impossibility. Which leads me to a personal story.

At the Pennsylvania Hospital we had an orderly named Sam who was deeply religious, and went around handing out religious tracts. He was pleasant and did a lot of work, so no one interfered. One day, I was walking in Times Square with my wife on one arm and my mother on the other. Looking ahead, I could see a crowd had formed around an orator on a soap box, who was none other than Sam. I said nothing, but as we drew closer, my mother exclaimed about it, and maneuvered the three of us up to the ringside to see the excitement. Sam stopped talking to the crowd, and shouted, "Hello, Doctor Fisher". So of course I replied, "Hello, Sam"; and the three of us kept walking down the street. After we had gone two blocks in silence, my mother abruptly stopped walking, stamped her foot, and said, "All right young man. Just who is this Sam?"

http://www.philadelphia-reflections.com/blog/2066.htm

Passage to India

Journalists intone that India has fallen behind in its infrastructure. Translation: it's often at risk of your life, to try to cross a street. The Indian road system is overwhelmed by an avalanche of rickshaws, tick tocks (motorcycle rickshaws), little cars, big cars, buses, trucks and motorcycles. All vehicles seem to be driven by teenaged maniacs, honking their horns and driving straight at you; the motor accident rate in India is among the worst in the world. It's not just a theory. One tour bus we were riding bashed into a motorcyclist, and just kept on going even though the passengers yelled and banged on the windows. Conclusion: airplanes and trains are the only reasonably comfortable ways to travel in India today. In another twenty years, things will surely improve or India must strangle, but right now you better save your pennies to afford the Palace on Wheels. That's a tourist train making a continuous loop through the main tourist attractions of central India, beginning and ending in New Delhi every Wednesday.

Palace on Wheel Train

Taj Mahal

You would have to be pretty aloof to avoid acknowledging the other seven passengers who share with you: one bedroom railroad car, two houseboys and a living room. And you soon enough know the busload (thirty passengers) in your guide group. Ours was the Pink Group, definitely not named for its political leanings. With that group, you also share a bar car, arranged in a facing circle of overstuffed furniture, (just as you see extended families in Bollywood movies), a sitting in one of the dining cars, and one tour bus with a Pink sign in the window. Thus organized, the twenty-car train with three trailing buses carries a hundred tourists with well-practiced efficiency in a style which claims to treat each passenger as a maharajah. While it is true these modern rajahs do not have three hundred concubines or twelve wives, the briefest reflection confirms that no sane man would want twelve wives or more than, say, twenty concubines. So the tourist's condition could arguably be held superior to that of any real maharajah.

The central point at the moment, however, is that the nature of this brief collection of strangers lends itself to gossip and reckless self-description, sort of like a rolling girls' boarding school. There's really nothing much to talk about except each other, and there are only eight in a conversation group.

While it was hard to overlook the mixed-ethnicity elderly couple in our midst, it was of course the ladies of the party who quickly assembled the essential bits of intelligence available. These two, an elderly Indian man

The Pink Group

with a broad smile and broader paunch, plus a thin wisp of a little white lady with the grace and social command of a duchess, had been friends in a Canadian nursing home where their children had placed them, had both lost their spouses, and then eloped to freedom. By escaping from the hateful nursing home they saved $9000 a month, so it really must have been a pretty upscale CCRC, or retirement village. In Canada there is lots of snow, cozy like an igloo all winter, but unquestionably confining. A little bit of scientific back-ground allowed me to estimate the life expectancy of these two to be about eight more years, or perhaps seven if you subtract the dismal last year that everyone would be glad to skip. These two had apparently counted up their resources and decided to make a dash for freedom to spend their last seven years in playland while they had the chance. The ladies in our group obviously thought this adventure was just about the most exciting thing ever, and grinned approvingly at every detail. Although our travel group overall seemed to have its fair share of boors, no one, absolutely no one was boorish enough to ask if there had been a wedding. Like pimpled teenagers, the two would slip their hands together with the hope that if they didn't look at their hands, no one else would notice. So, from time to time, the gentleman would slide his hand onto her thigh. And she, with the practiced skill of a high school cheerleader, would wait thirty seconds and with a big smile aimed at no one in particular, brush his hand away. She was having a perfectly wonderful time because she knew very well that every other lady was watching every movement.

Palace Train

Ben Franklin moved with the fast set in Paris in his eighties, and in fact probably moved with a fast set where ever he was at any age. He seldom discussed the topic directly except in that famous letter to his son which concluded, "And son, they are so grateful". In our present society which claims such infinite sophistication, Ben might now reflect on the pressures of inheritance laws which thwart re-marriages. Or on age-related indifference to complicating children which some couples need more than others. In fact, Franklin's famous letter to his (illegitimate) son enumerates a list of advantages of love affairs with older women which could just as easily have been listed by John Milton or Cotton Mather. At least one gentleman has given the opinion that Franklin was all mischievous talk, and no action. But I dunno. That remark about how grateful they are, surely carries a tone of personal experience.

http://www.philadelphia-reflections.com/blog/2089.htm

Paying for Assisted Living

Everyone knows Americans are living thirty years longer because of improvements in health care, and some grumpy people are waiting with glee to see if Obamacare will put a stop to that sort of thing. It must be left to actuaries to tell us whether the nation saves money or not by delaying the inevitable costs of terminal illness. But one consequence has already made its appearance: people are entering retirement villages in their eighties rather than their seventies. Presumably, people in their seventies are feeling too well to consider a CCRC, although other explanations are possible.

Accordingly, a great many CCRCs are seen to be building new wings dedicated to "assisted living". A cynic might surmise there must be some hidden insurance reimbursement advantages to doing so, but the CCRCs are surely responding to some kind of increased demand when they make multi-million dollar capital expenditures. Assisted living is a polite term for people with strokes or Alzheimers Disease, or some other condition making it hard to walk, or, as the grisly saying goes, perform the activities of daily living. One really elegant place in Delaware has suites with servants quarters, but for most people the only affordable option is to be in a room designed around the idea of assisting an invalid. It's generally smaller and more austere, but fitted out with railings and bars and special knobs. Meals generally have to be supplied by room service.

CCRCs

Not everyone is destined to have a protracted period of decline, but it's fairly frequent and universally feared, so it's a comfort to know your present residence is attached to a wing which provides for it. The question is how to pay for it. There are two main approaches currently in use, adapted to the limited financial resources of the aged and the particularities of CCRC arrangements.

Obama Care

In the first arrangement, there is no increased charge for moving to assisted living, which helps overcome resistance to going there. However, the monthly maintenance charge for others who remain behind in "ambulatory living" is increased, usually about 20%, to provide funding for those who eventually need special assistance. That's a financial pooling arrangement, sort of an insurance plan, and like all insurance it has a tendency to increase usage unnecessarily. It also increases the cost to those who enter the CCRC at an earlier age, because they make more monthly payments before they use them. Although the monthly premium probably goes up as the costs rise with inflation, there may be some savings hidden in applying an earlier payment stream at a lower rate. That's called "present value" accounting, but like all accounting, its unspoken advantages and disadvantages lie in a gamble on unknown future inflation.

In the other common financial arrangement, you pay as you go, when and only if you actually use the assisted living quarters. Because of the likely limit to resources, there is usually an attached agreement to garnishee the initial entrance deposit if available funds prove insufficient. The one thing which won't happen is being thrown out in the snow for non-payment; there's a law prohibiting that. Bigger apartments with large initial returnable deposits are of course better off paying list prices. Those with smaller apartments may have smaller deposits, and favor payment by a percent withdrawal. Some places haven't thought this through and offer no choice. In that case, more attention should be paid to those list prices and the percentage markup from audited cost. Better still is to have a free choice of both options, with cost transparency.

The remaining choice is between two CCRCs with differing options, made at the time you enter. The Obamacare fuss has made a lot of people acquainted with "adverse risk selection", which is largely based on the idea that an individual has a better idea of his health future than an institution does, since that includes family history as well as earlier health experiences. But in general, a young healthy person is going to live longer without needing assisted living than an old geezer who going to need it pretty soon. A hidden adverse incentive is created for younger healthier people to avoid the place, and come back in ten years, providing they become aware of the underlying reason the monthly fee is somewhat higher than in some competitive CCRC and possibly even if they don't. At the other end of the age spectrum, an incentive is created to go into assisted living quarters a little earlier in life, generally regarded as an undesirable choice.

All of this calculation can seem pretty overwhelming to an elderly person who isn't entirely comfortable with the CCRC idea, in the first place. Rest assured that everything has to be paid for somehow, and after you die you won't care what choice has been made. If you trust the institution to have your best interests in mind, the only consideration of real importance is whether your money will last you out. The institution cares about that even more than you do, so they aren't likely to offer any unrealistic choices.

America has had a ninety-year romance with insurance, because it is so comforting to be secure and oblivious to finances. This is just another example of the principle at work, but while I'm not so sure about it, we're essentially all in this together.

http://www.philadelphia-reflections.com/blog/2112.htm

Heavenly House

While prosperous people, on deciding to enter a retirement community, are often heard to say they are tired of managing a big house, it can also be noticed that people who get the foreign travel bug usually drift around to see the palaces, castles and estates of kings and emperors. The king's bathroom plumbing is a stop on most tours. Places like Buckingham Palace, the Vatican, the Temples of Karnak, Fortresses of Mogul Conquerors of India, or similar places in Cambodia, are all vast looming piles of stone dedicated to the memory of departed leaders who Had it All. That's probably all you

Father Divine House

need know, to understand that Americans who have it all tend to build huge show places, too. A great many do discover the castles to become just too much bother. Safe protection and privacy are somewhat separate issues, reasons given for putting up with a big place past the time the thrill has worn off. Perhaps such jaded feelings appear at the end of the wealth cycle. Nevertheless with enough affluence, if you had unlimited money and inclination, where around Philadelphia would you put a dream palace, one built for a modern Maharajah? Answer: close to Conshohocken.

Philadelphia Country Club

The Schuylkill takes a sharp bend at Conshohocken, because it flows around a big cliff on the west side of the river. It was there the White Steel Company built the first wire suspension bridge in the world, as distinguished from cable (twisted wire) suspension bridges invented by Roebling at Trenton. The bridge was swept away by a flood, the steel mill replaced by the Alan J. Wood Steel Company. Alan Wood prospered mightily, and built his mansion ("Woodmont") on 75 acres on the top of the big rock on the west side of the Schulylkill, in such a way he could watch the smoke rising from his factory down below at the foot of the cliff. The Philadelphia Country Club is across the road from Alan Wood's mansion, with fairways clinging to the cliffs, a Gun Club for trap shooters who want to aim away from houses and toward mountainsides, and a cliff-top road leading straight for Gladwyne between dozens of mansions with five-acre lots. Down the hill, however, rocky projections force the road to funnel into a winding crooked road which ends up near the filling stations of Conshohocken, passing ancient farm structures on the way. Railroads and expressways tend to fill the valley, the old White bridge is gone, and two distinct cultures are within a few hundred oblivious yards of each other. To the west stretches the Main Line, now filled with houses almost as large as the mansion, but air conditioned and filled with other modern amenities. Seventy acres of lawn are nice, but it's a lot of grass to cut.

The Alan Wood Steel Company had a hard time in 1929, recovered somewhat after World War II, and then declined to the point where Lukens and Phoenix Steel took over. And then Indians from India took over the lot, forming part of the largest steel complex in the world, now headquartered abroad. In 1952, one of Father Divine's religious followers named John Devoute gave Father the Wood mansion; which then became the new headquarters of his religious sect. He died in 1965 but Mother Divine still lives there in stately and tasteful semi-seclusion. The grounds of the estate are beautifully tended by various of the twenty-five attendants of Mother. Father's mausoleum is near the house.

The house itself is patterned after Biltmore in Asheville, NC, although perhaps only a quarter as large. Just inside its portecachier, the oak paneled living room has a ceiling 45 feet high, and many oriental rugs. There is a music room, off to the side of which is Father's former office, bearing a strong resemblance to the Oval Office in the White House in Washington. As planned, the

Mother and Father Divine

living room window looks down the valley to the site of the old steel mills, although when the trees are leafed out it may be difficult to see. The dining table probably seats forty people, although the paneled dining room was fitted with electronics and used to broadcast sermons to religious adherents across the country. In the living room are testimonies to the many who seemed to rise from the dead, or who had their blinded sight restored, or who were crippled but enabled to walk. The attendants take visitors on tours, but Mother Divine likes to meet them, coming down the sweeping staircase without noticeably showing her age. The greeting of "Peace" replaces the usual "hello" and "goodbye".

At one time, the Religion housed a large number of single women in several hotels, and the invested proceeds of their work as domestics still supports the Religion. The religion frowned on gambling, drinking, smoking and sex. However, celibacy inevitably leads to decline of numbers, particularly evident since the death of the founder.

http://www.philadelphia-reflections.com/blog/2126.htm

Ageing Owners, Ageing Property

Kiyohiko Nishimura is currently the Deputy Governor of the Bank of Japan (BOJ), and as such is expected to have wise things to say about finances, as indeed he does. Japan has a far older culture than the United States, and a botanical uniqueness growing out of the glaciers avoiding it, many thousands of years ago. But its latitude is approximately the same as ours, and its modern culture is affected by the deliberate effort of the Emperor to westernize the nation, following its "opening up" by our own Commodore Matthew Perry in 1852. Perhaps a more important relationship between the two cultures for present purposes is that Japan has been suffering from the current deep recession for fourteen years longer than we have. We don't want to repeat that performance, but we can certainly learn from it.

Kiyohiko Nishimura

Mr. Nishimura lays great stress on the ageing of the Japanese population because in all nations, houses are mainly purchased by young newly-weds, and sold by that same generation years later as they prepare to retire. If a nation has an elderly population, it can expect a general lowering of house prices some day, reflecting too many sellers leaving the market at the same time. The buyers of those houses are competing with other young people, so the simultaneous bulges and dips of population at later stages combine to have major effects on housing prices. At the moment, younger couples are having fewer children as a result of women postponing the first one. Nishimura goes on to reflect that something like the same is true of stocks and bonds, although at age levels five or ten years later. One implication is that retirement of our own World War II baby boom is about to depress American home prices, which will likely stay lowered for 10-20 more years. Furthermore, our stock market will have its similar effect, stretching the depression out by as much as 5-15 years. The Japanese stock market has been a gloomy place to be during the past fifteen years, and by these lights might continue in the doldrums for another five or so. Meanwhile, our own situation predicts an additional generation of struggle while Japan is recovering. It's best not to apply these ideas too closely, of course, but surely somebody in our government ought to dig around in the data, at least telling us why we ain't goin' to repeat this pattern. Please.

Perhaps because they eat so much rice and fish, the Japanese already have a longer life expectancy than Americans do, but in terms of outliving your assets, that's not wholly advantageous, the way a love of golf might be. The best our nation might be able to do is to examine some of our premises about housing construction.

Commodore Matthew Perry and Japan

The house walls of the town of Kyoto are sometimes made of waxed paper, which seems to work fairly well. While no one advocates going quite so far, we might think a second time about building the big hulking masonry houses so favored in our affluent suburbs. Such cumbersome building materials almost dictate custom building, and strongly discourage mass production. How likely are such fortresses to survive in the real estate markets of fifty years from now? Judging from my home town, not too well. Haddonfield boasts it has been around since 1701, and there are at most three or four of its houses which have survived that long. We favor great hulking Victorian frame houses, with a good many bedrooms unoccupied, and high drafty ceilings, very large window openings and little original insulation. The heating arrangements have gone from fireplaces, to coal furnaces, to oil, and lately to natural gas. The meter reader who checks my consumption every month tells me that almost all the houses now have gas heat, so almost all the houses are using their second or third heating plant, along with their eighth or tenth roof, and thirty coats of paint. This kind of maintenance is not prohibitively expensive, but just wait until the plumbing starts to go, and leak, and freeze, with attendant plastering, carpentry and painting. Our schools and transportation are excellent, so we have location, location, location. But when the plumbing, heating and roofing start to require financial infusions all at once, you get tear-downs. A tear-down is a new house in which a specialist builder buys the old house, tears it down, and looks for a buyer to commission the new house on an old plot of land. Right now, there appear to be six or eight such Haddonfield houses, torn down and looking for a buyer to commission a new house on that location, location. If we repeat the Japanese experience, there will be some unhappy people, somewhere. And that will include the neighbors like me, who generally do not relish languishing vacant lots next door, but fear what the new one will be like.

Greenfield Hall

The thought has to occur to somebody that building the whole town of less substantial materials in the first place would be worth investigation, replacing the houses every forty years when the major stuff wears out. At the present, when a town of several thousand houses has five or six tear-downs, the neighbors would not tolerate replacing tear-downs with insubstantial cardboard boxes. Seeing what has happened to inner-city school systems, the neighbors would be uneasy about "affordable housing" built in place of stately old Homes of Pride. In time, that might lead to a deterioration of one of the two pillars of location, location – the schools – and hence to a massive loss of asset value. And yet when those houses empty out the school children, leaving only retirees in place, the schools will not be worth much to the owners or in time to anybody else. There's an unfortunate tendency for local political control to migrate into the hands of local real estate brokers, so you had better be sure any bright new proposal is tightly buttressed with facts.

The only real hope for an evolution in this obsolete system may lie in the schools of architecture, strengthened perhaps by some research grants. Countless World Fairs have displayed the proud products of their imaginative thinking, but mostly to no avail. Perhaps the ideas are not yet ripe, but since it would take more than a generation to create a useful demonstration project of whatever does become ripe for decision, let's start thinking about some innovative suburban designs, right now.

http://www.philadelphia-reflections.com/blog/2176.htm

Labyrinth, Episcopalian Version

The Reverend Diana Carroll, Assistant Rector of Holy Trinity Church on Rittenhouse Square, recently addressed the Right Angle Club about the labyrinth to be found there. The fact is, it is there because she put it there, where it is open to the public one Saturday afternoon a month. There are half a dozen other labyrinths in Philadelphia Churches, mostly forgotten, so this is a revival of a custom rather than the invention of one. St. Asaph's on City Line Avenue, St. Stephen's at 10th and Market and a few others have them, mostly neglected and forgotten. Reverend Carroll admits to importing the tradition to Holy Trinity, persuading everybody in charge to nurture it, and setting aside one

Reverend Diana Carroll

Saturday afternoon for the public to visit each month. Labyrinths differ in their design; this one copies the design within Chartres Cathedral in France. In England, labyrinths are much more popular, and have other designs.

Contrary to popular belief, a labyrinth only has one entrance, which is also its only exit. The visitor goes in, goes round and round and comes to a dead end, and then goes back out the same way. There's no great problem about getting lost; the confusing puzzles of ancient lore are not labyrinths, they are mazes. Whether with walls or simply lines on the floor, labyrinths are

Labyrinth

designed for meditation and symbolism. It's possible to bump into other people on the way out, it's possible to be struck by the symbolism of reaching the center of things, it's possible to imagine the human condition of getting into things and then getting yourself out. Diana Carroll says the labyrinth evokes the image of feminism to her, entering or leaving the uterus. That thought might not have occurred to everyone else, but agreement isn't central to appreciating labyrinths.

The Nazca lines, best seen from an airplane over Chile, evoked the image of labyrinths to several Right Angle members. Those lines are a couple thousand years old, in a decidedly non-Christian environment at the time. Forty five centuries B.C. could safely be judged to precede Christianity, so it becomes clear that this concept is discontinuous, popping up in many minds in many circumstances. Some theologians might well contend this proves that meditation labyrinths are therefore not part of

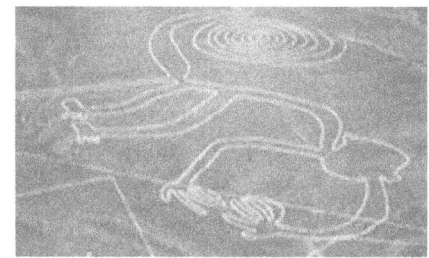
Nazca Lines

any fixed religious doctrine. But others, with equal justice, might say it proves that labyrinths are part of the essential nature of contemplative man. Or as in Reverend Carroll's case, woman.

http://www.philadelphia-reflections.com/blog/2090.htm

Children's Scholarship Fund of Philadelphia (2)

Because the Right Angle Club makes donations to the Children's Scholarship Fund, representatives are asked to come discuss it with us from time to time. We recently had such a visit, resulting in a growing understanding of what the fund accomplishes. Briefly

Children's Scholarship Fund

stated, their scholarship winners have a 95% record of graduating from high school, and a 90% record of going to college. That compares very favorably with the average Philadelphia public school enrollee, who only achieves a 50% record of graduation.

That's got to be a good record, achieved by selecting the scholarship winners by random lottery; obviously, that's better still. It's not quite random, however, because the siblings from a winner's family are also awarded a scholarship. Let's repeat: the winners are not selected because of talent, IQ or achievement test. Nor are they followed, to see if they actually go to school or do their homework. Therefore, these children are definitely not selected because of either merit or diligence. They are just poor kids from Philadelphia, randomly selected by lottery. So what accounts for their markedly superior record of graduation and admission to college? It just about has to be related to either the parents or the school, and mostly it seems to be the quality of the school.

The parents have to be sufficiently motivated to contribute up to $500 yearly co-payment, because that accounts for about 20% of the extra cost. A variety of other community sources account for 40%, and 40% is matched by the generous donor and originator of the idea. When the alternative for a poor family is free public school, a $500 cost really is an incentive to get something back for the money.

But most likely the main difference in outcome is due to the excellence and effort of the school. About two hundred private schools in Philadelphia are carefully selected as eligible participants, and of course there is the invisible threat of withdrawing schools from the list if things don't work out. It's thus pretty hard to escape giving sole credit to the excellence of the teachers and schools, when the contribution of the parents is mostly to demand that the students submit to it. So, like it or lump it, this scholarship fund is a social experiment in whether inner-city academic performance will improve if you improve the schools, and essentially do nothing else. And raising the performance from 50% failure to nearly 100% success, certainly emerges almost totally as an achievement of a better school system. When the failing public school system compares so poorly while spending more money, the point is proven to most people. Note to politicians: fix the $#@&^# schools, and promptly.

With this point so definitively made, it is indeed possible that some of the ideas of the originator were a little off the mark. It is commonly argued by opponents of school vouchers that merit promotion of the students, or merit-based scholarships, or the creation of centers of excellence all have the potential for siphoning off the best students, thus worsening the remaining academic environment, the incentives for the teachers, and the discipline – for everybody else. This experimental program dramatically proves that any such effects are overwhelmed by improving the schools in inexpensive ways. Most ambitious parents are already determined to move their children to better schools if they can find them, no matter what is done – or not done – to help substandard pupils; the day of bewildered immigrant rural peasants arriving on our shores is over.

Fixing the elementary schools is thus exposed as a purely political problem; kick out the politicians with the unions they are protecting, and the job is nearly done. After all, children below the fourth grade are mostly sweet little confections, ready to flower if you remove impediments. The inner-city schools from fourth to twelfth are a somewhat more difficult issue, mostly because of their hormone content. The home environment is probably more important at that age, and changing whole cultures is very difficult. But the Philadelphia School System was once a source of great pride, and the Philadelphia Catholic School System was once the best in America. Somehow, the suburban secondary school system is falling down on its job as unchallenged exemplar, coasting on invidious comparisons with the inner city. It's high time the suburban schools stopped preening themselves, and stopped coddling the outrageous behavior and low academic standards the situation promotes in both students and teachers. Let each one of these places adopt a sister school in the inner city and help it out. The college admissions committees could help this happen a little by shifting their preferences to suburban private schools, unless or until the suburban high schools pull up their socks.

From time to time, someone angry about education expresses the wish for a deep economic depression or a massive world war, or both. Please. What's needed here is competition.

http://www.philadelphia-reflections.com/blog/2091.htm

Adrift With The Living Constitution

Former Congressman Joe Sestak visited the Franklin Inn Club recently, describing his experiences with the Tea Party movement. Since Senator Patrick Toomey, the man who defeated him in the 2010 election, is mostly a Libertarian, and Senator Arlen Specter who also lost has switched parties twice, all three candidates in the Pennsylvania senatorial election displayed major independence from party dominance, although in different ways. Ordinarily, gerrymandering and political machine politics result in a great many "safe" seats, where a representative or a Senator has more to fear from rivals in his own party than from his opposition in the other party; this year, things seem to be changing in our area. Pennsylvania is somehow in the vanguard of a major national shift in party politics, although it is unclear whether a third

Senator Joe Sestak

party is about to emerge, or whether the nature of the two party system is about to change in some other way.

For his part, Joe Sestak (formerly D. Representative from Delaware County) had won the Democratic senatorial nomination against the wishes of the party leaders, who had previously promised the nomination to incumbent Senator Specter in reward for Specter's switching from the Republican to Democratic party. For Vice-Admiral Sestak, USN (ret.) it naturally stings a little that he won the nomination without leadership support, but still came reasonably close to winning the general election without much enthusiasm within his party. He clearly believes he would have beaten Toomey if the party leaders had supported him. It rather looks as though the Democratic party leadership would rather lose the election to the Republicans than lose control of nominations, which are their real source of power. Controlling nominations is largely a process of persuading unwelcome contenders to drop out of the contest. Sestak is therefore making a large number of thank- you visits after the election, and clearly has his ears open for signs of what the wandering electorate might think of his future candidacy.

America clearly prefers a two-party system to both the dictatorial tendencies of a one-party system, as well as to European multi- party arrangements, such as run-offs or coalitions. A two-party system blunts the edges of extreme partisanship, eventually moving toward moderate candidates in the middle, in order to win a winner-take-all election. Therefore, our winner-take-all rules are the enforcement mechanism for a two-party system. Our deals and bargains are made in advance of the election, where the public can express an

Senator Patrick Toomey

opinion. In multi-party systems the deals are made after the election where the public can't see what's going on, and such arrangements are historically unstable, sometimes resulting in a victory by a minority fringe with violently unpopular policies. In our system, a new third-party mainly serves as a mechanism for breaking up one of the major parties, to reformulate it as a two-party system with different composition. Proportional representation is defended by European politicians as something which promotes "fairness". Unfortunately, it's pretty hard to find anything in politics anywhere which is sincerely devoted to fairness.

Going far back in history one of the great theorists of legislative politics was the Roman Senator Pliny the Younger, who wrote books in Latin about how to manipulate a voting system. For him, parties were only temporary working arrangements about individual issues, a situation where he recommended "insincere voting" as a method for winning a vote even if you lacked a majority in favor of it. Over the centuries, other forms of party coalitions have emerged in nations attempting to make democracy workable. Indeed, a "republic" itself can be seen as a mechanism devised for retaining popular control in an electorate grown too large for the chaos and unworkability of pure town hall democracy. A republic is a democracy which has been somewhat modified to make it workable. Our founding fathers knew

Senator Specter

this from personal experience, and never really considered pure democracy even in the Eighteenth century.

The two main actors in shaping the American Republic were George Washington and James Madison. Madison was young, scholarly and largely unknown; Washington was old, famous, and insecure about his lack of academic political education. Both of them knew very well that if Washington really wanted something he was going to have it; what mainly restrained him was fear of looking foolish. But he hated partisanship and conniving, partly as a result of having been the victim of General Mifflin and the Conway Cabal. Washington hated political parties and anything resembling them; Madison was young and uncertain, and briefly surrendered the point. It took about two years of real-life governing for Madison to conclude that political parties were absolutely essential to getting something accomplished. In this he experienced for the first time those unwelcome "pressures from the home state", with Thomas Jefferson determined to thwart Alexander Hamilton, and Patrick Henry thundering and denouncing any hesitation in going for the jugular vein of opponents. Madison was deeply concerned with making his new nation a success, and eventually joined Jefferson in the Virginia policy of opposing banks, cities and manufacturing. When Washington saw that Madison was committed to this course, he never spoke to him again. For Washington, honesty was always the best policy, and personal honor is never regained once it is lost. The compromise of 1790 was particularly vexing to their relationship, when Washington's honor and personal finances were used as bargaining chips for moving the nation's capital opposite Mount Vernon on the Potomac River, in return for placating Hamilton and Robert Morris with the assumption of state revolutionary war debts.

Legislative partisan politics took a violent turn in 1811, when 34-year old Henry Clay was

Henry Clay 1811

elected to his first term as member of the House of Representatives. The Senate was less prestigious than the House in those days, and Clay had spent his time as a senator studying the landscape of the House, before he made his big move upward. Up until that moment, the role of Speaker was that of mediator and administrator of the rules, partisanship was considered a shameful thing in a Speaker. Young Clay was elected Speaker on the first day of the first session after he moved to the House as a member. Seniority was brushed aside, and this newcomer took over. It takes only a moment's reflection to surmise that a lot of politics had taken place before the House convened. Not only that, but Clay immediately added the power of the Speaker to appoint committee chairmen, to the invisible powers of majority leader. The office of majority leader had not yet been created, but it was not long in emerging that anyone who could assemble enough votes for Speaker was also able to make highly partisan choices for Committee Chairs. Eventually, the seniority system was imposed in part as a reaction to perceived abuses of Speaker power. It is worth a digression to reflect on the role of any seniority system, which as it is clearly seen in labor-management industrial relations, serves to deprive management of promotion power, usually substituting seniority for selection by merit. In the case of the Speaker, the seniority system catapults the power of the Speaker over that of every member of his caucus. To rise in a seniority system for committee chairmen, a member must first be appointed to a desirable committee – by the Speaker, or by his instructed favorites on the appointment committee. It puts in the hands of the Speaker or his agents the power to humiliate a member by ignoring his seniority; the other members know immediately what that means. To understand the power of this threat, reflect on Woodrow Wilson's famous observation that "Congress in committee, is Congress at work."

Soon after Henry Clay made his dramatic moves, Martin van Buren extended the idea of partisan party politics to the actual election of Congressmen. Much of the whoopla and deceptiveness of subsequent campaigns was invented by Andrew Jackson's vice president. And that included their own deal, in which van Buren worked for Jackson's election in return for a promise that he would be the successor President. After that came the election of 1848, in which William Henry Harrison was elected as a man born in a log cabin. When, in fact he had been born in one of the largest mansions in Virginia. That had been approximately George Washington's residence description, too, but it is hard to see Old Stone Face lowering himself to accept any office unless it was offered unanimously.

Compare that with the campaign financing episode which created the urban political machine. The Philadelphia traction king Wm. L. Elkins was narrowly concerned with building street car lines along with his business associate P.A.B. Widener; Widener had been a city politician before he got into street cars. One or the other of these two approached the Mayor of Philadelphia with the complaint that it interfered with building street car lines to have to bribe every bartender on every street corner. So he made a proposal. It wasn't the money that bothered him, because he could just raise trolley fares to cover it, it was the protracted delays. So, how would it be if the trolley company just delivered a big lump-sum bribe to the mayor.

That would give enormous political power to the party boss through the power to distribute or withhold the boodle to party workers. And it would save the trolley company lots of time, while not costing any more than the "retail graft" system. Since then, just about every urban political machine in the country has been largely financed through the macing of utilities.

The downward trend of serial modifications to the Philadelphia Constitution of 1787, should be clear enough without further illustration. If the Tea Parties aren't mad about it, they should be. More likely, however, they are mainly mad about the modern pinacle of sly tinkerings, plainly displayed on TV during the enactment of the Obama Health Bill. The point was repeated for emphasis in the Dodd-Frank financial bill, in case it is ever claimed to have been accidental. In both cases, 2000 page bills were prepared out of sight, and thrust before the Congress with orders to enact them in four hours. If that's representative government, perhaps we ought to go back to having a King.

http://www.philadelphia-reflections.com/blog/2097.htm

Anatomy of an Urban Political Machine

The Franklin Inn Club meets every Monday morning to discuss the news, and recently it discussed the upcoming local political campaign. The discussion went on for fifteen minutes before a newcomer asked if we were talking about the primary or the general election. The question was met with broad smiles all around, because of course we were talking about the primary. Voter registration is 6:1 in favor of the Democrats in Philadelphia, so the general election is just a required formality. The election, that is, consists only of the Democrat primary; election of the Democrat nominee in the general election is a foregone conclusion. Someone idly remarked on the number of

One Big Family

politicians who are blood relatives of other politicians, someone else said that was true of union officers, too. So, skipping from the inside baseball of the election, we took a little time to discuss the anatomy of an urban political machine.

The first step in consolidating control of a city by a political machine is to eliminate the issue of the general election by making the other party's chances seem hopeless. That converts an election which typically turns out 40% of the voters into an exclusively primary election, turning out 20% of the voters, or even less in an off-year. In some "safe" districts a winner needs far less than 10% of the eligible vote to win.

The second step is to run as a prominent member of a local ethnic or religious group, preferably the largest of such groups within the district. If possible, election is almost assured by being the sole candidate associated with the largest ethnic group. Here's where family connections work for you. If your father held the same seat, or some other family member had been prominent in the district, it helps assure everybody that you are really an ethnic member, and not just someone whose name sounds as though it would be. Your relative will know who is important in locally local politics, the members of large families, or people known to be the "go-to guy".

Assembling all that, the final step is to get everyone else who is a member of the ethnic group to drop out of the primary, and to encourage other ethnic groups to field as many candidates as possible, splitting up their vote. Getting other members of your religious group to drop out, consists of having your relative approach them and tell them to wait their turn. The implicit promise underneath that advice is probably next to worthless, unless it is specific and witnessed, and the other fellow's ability to deliver it is credible. If all else fails, the resistant opponent is muscled in some way, verbally at first, and then increasingly threatening. The consequence of this ethnic/religious influence is more involvement in government by clergy than is healthy for either one of them. Now, that's about all there is to achieving permanent incumbency, but the minority party should be mentioned, as well as the flow of money.

the Parking Authority

It quite often happens that the minority party in the big city, hopeless in its own election chances, finds itself with a Governor and/or Legislature of their party. The patronage of state jobs becomes available to the foot soldiers who have no chance of local election. Much of the wrangling within state legislatures revolves around whether appointive patronage jobs should be lodged in state agencies, or local ones; at the moment, the Parking Authority and the Port Authorities figure prominently as jobs for which a local Republican could aspire. The coin of this trade is maintaining influence in the state nominating process, and paying off with increased voter turn-out in elections which have no local effect but may be important at the state or national level. Since party dominance at state and national levels changes frequently, the local machine finds it useful to continue this system. Where they have nothing to lose in local elections, they may even encourage it.

Money is the mother's milk of politics. Except for safe districts no one can get elected without it. And various degrees of corruption provide money to be "spread around" the clubhouse, sometimes to induce people to drop out of primary races, sometimes to console "sacrifice" candidates who run hopeless campaigns just to make the party look good, and sometimes just to enrich the undeserving. The politically connected parts of the legal profession participate a good deal in the flow of funds, sometimes in order to get government legal work, sometimes to obtain judgeships, sometimes to launder the money for clients. One particularly lurid story circulates that professional sports teams are expected to make seven-figure contributions in return for lavish new stadium construction, from which they in turn are able to generate various sorts of compensating revenue.

But, as the old story goes, if you eat lunch with a tiger, the tiger eats last.

http://www.philadelphia-reflections.com/blog/2114.htm

Perpetuities

Although some churches and mummies are well preserved after thousands of years, and no doubt a few corporations do last a century, the fact is most of them don't last very long. Most new corporations go bankrupt within ten years, and only one (General Electric) of the original thirty members of the Dow-Jones Industrial Average existed in 1900. Members of the Dow may seem the biggest and best, but in fact live on a slippery slope. Not-for-profits, like churches, may do somewhat better, although the handful who approach perpetual status may be rare exceptions. One big reason not to leave a major bequest to any of them, may well be that most will not survive. While we are on this subject, the same reasoning applies to the stock in for-profit corporations. Since few of them thrive for more than seventy-five years, the idea of buying their stock, holding it forgotten in a safety-deposit box, and passing it on intact to

Johnathan Edwards

heirs, is probably doomed to investment failure. The oldest stockholder company in America is called the Proprietors of West Jersey, founded in 1676 but still meeting once or twice a year. It would be moderately interesting to know how well this investment performed over the years, but Google sounds like a better bet offhand. Just don't hold it too long.

Cotton Mathers

There may be a connection between success as a non-profit and success in the merciless marketplace. Those who have compiled statistics will tell you that steadily withdrawing more than 4% a year from an endowment portfolio, sooner or later leads to a day when there is nothing left. Most trustees expect better results than that, and most managers of non-profits will need more than that, no matter how big the pile was when they started. Sooner or later, markets will decline, mistakes will be made, and the endowment will be exhausted by "emergency" withdrawals which relentlessly withdraw more than 4%. This pitiful decline might be avoided by gathering the managers of influential non-profits together, giving them a stern lecture, and somehow forcing them to live within their means, but offhand nothing sounds more futile. Jonathan Edwards and Cotton Mather were said to be good at haranguing. But since it must be obvious that non-profits usually survive by constantly soliciting fresh

endowment funds, what would be the matter with taking a direct approach to that goal. Why not just state in advance that the institution is only intended to do its good work for say fifty years, and then it must turn its residuals over to somebody else? Not many endowments have been limited to a lifetime of fifty years, but in those who have done so, the experience seems to be that most of them immediately set about to raise additional funds to keep the institution from disappearing. The American Enterprise Institute in Washington, for example, started out dispensing about a million dollars a year; last year it dispensed over $30 million. Whether he intended it or not, the message

Mr. Olin transmitted was not that think tanks are only good for thirty years. He told his executors in effect, "You have some seed capital with which to start a think tank. Whether it lasts longer than fifty years, is now up to you."

http://www.philadelphia-reflections.com/blog/2131.htm

Lowering the Taxes on Corporations

In the early years of the 21st Century, Ireland lowered taxes on corporate profits to a 12.5% rate, far lower than neighboring countries. Whatever else it did, it promptly encouraged corporations in Germany, Denmark, the United Kingdom and other neighbors – to move headquarters to Ireland where taxes were so low. Ireland is primarily rural, and a housing shortage developed in the cities as workers migrated to take advantage of the new jobs. Home prices went through the roof, mortgage applications overwhelmed local banks, who promptly re-sold mortgages to foreign banks. Sound familiar? It caused a housing bubble and then a horrendous international financial crisis. The European Union is financially and politically strained by the consequences, and threatened to break apart over it.

Irish Jig

That sounds pretty bad, and should be a lesson to others. What Canada and a number of the individual United States got out of it was mainly this: if you lower corporation taxes, it causes prosperity. And so it might, if politicians would do it gradually and moderately. Gradually and moderately are unfamiliar words in politics. Furthermore, there has long been a fundamental unfairness in taxing corporate profits twice – once when the profits are made, and a second time when dividends are paid to shareholders. But it is obviously dangerous business, particularly when the governments involved are inexperienced. Canadians started talking about lowering their taxes to 16.5%, and no one could say whether that is a safe level or not. Within weeks, twenty-nine states with Republican governors were sending up trial balloons about joining this movement, and Governor Mitch Daniels of Indiana was much in demand as a consultant, and maybe a Presidential candidate, because Indiana had lowered corporate taxation some time ago, with favorable results.

This was exactly the sort of behavior James Madison had in mind when he designed the United States Constitution; it gave the people a way of disciplining overbearing state governments. Raise our taxes, and we will move. So there are strong arguments that these governors are approaching the right thing, and equally strong indications that everybody had better be plenty careful how this is approached.

The basic idea is good; double taxation should stop, and there is nothing in Madison's Constitution to prevent the Governors from doing what they say they would like to do. So how's this for a suggestion: if this movement gets started, let's take the opportunity to reduce all corporate income taxation to zero. If everybody has the same zero rate, the incentive to migrate will disappear, and that's a good thing.

But if a major revenue source for the states disappears, what will take its place? At that moment of what would look like crisis, it would be time for a national reconsideration and revision of the tax codes. And that would be an even more desirable outcome, provided it is done in an orderly and sensible way.

http://www.philadelphia-reflections.com/blog/2064.htm

Causes of the 2007 Crash: Political and Technological

Dealing with a topic as complicated as the causes of the 2007 financial crisis, it's quite possible for two viewpoints to be entirely in agreement, until abruptly coming to different conclusions. In this paper, we consider the relative merits of blaming government housing subsidies in various forms, relative to blaming the unanticipated effects of the computer revolution. The subsidy argument has just been succinctly and effectively argued by a lawyer, Peter J. Wallison. Agreeing with every word he writes, I nevertheless hold the perspective that disruptive effects of the computer revolution were equally responsible, if not more so. Politics *versus* technology, choose your poison.

Federal Reserve

Mr. Wallison served as a lawyer in the financial loins of Washington, and thus has the perspective of a Reaganite who sees government as the main problem; with the significant distinction that his proposals for solution also lie in government corrective action, particularly "covered bonds" and step-wise privatization of the Federal Housing Authority (FHA). While agreeing with both reform proposals, my concern here is about too little general recognition in the analysis of how vulnerable the banking system has become, to revolutions made possible by even primitive computers of the 1960s. Such revolutions soon grew many times magnified by the inexpensive high-speed internet. If that analysis is correct, it predicts mere legislative action for the housing industry will prove inadequate; banking has taken a radical new direction.

Mr. Wallison's argument in the January 3, 2011 edition of the *Wall Street Journal* is admirably succinct. He points out the New Deal Federal Reserve deliberately suppressed interest rates to the benefit of the housing industry, but made a significant exception for the Savings and Loans. (It was forced to abandon that approach by the innovation of money market funds, in turn made feasible by widespread adoption of the IBM 360 computer.) When the S&Ls collapsed, that segment of the market was awarded to the GSEs (Fannie and Freddy Mac, insured by FHA). In 1992, Congress imposed the goal of promoting "affordable housing" on the GSEs, which is to say the subsidization of "subprime" (i.e. high risk) mortgages. By 2007, half of all mortgages were subprime, and by September 7, 2008 Fan and Fred were insolvent, effectively replaced by the Federal

Reserve (i.e. the taxpayers) as the final guarantor against national insolvency. It will take a decade to restore the economy from its present setback, but Mr. Wallison's proposals do indeed have some chance of eventually leading to a viable economy. **He proposes** the threshold for "jumbo" mortgages be reduced by $50,000 every six months until mortgages are effectively privatized. **And** he also suggests we create a pool of mortgage assets as security for a bond issue, thus privatizing existing mortgages in the way Europeans describe as a "covered bond" system. Go ahead, do it; it might work, and nothing else is on offer.

Meanwhile take a look at banks; we seemingly can't get along without them. But other institutions are undermining them, with cheaper products made possible by computers. For two centuries, banks transformed short-term borrowing into long-term loans; no one else could do it. It's a simple idea, and it works, that a constant or even rising pool level can be maintained by a steady inflow of short-term deposits. But it is risky; the risk is that some event will precipitate a sudden rush of withdrawals, a run on the bank. Sooner or later, the law of averages catches up. The risk is real, it happens every few years. A price in the form of interest must be imposed to maintain

IBM 360 Computer

reserves against occasional bank runs, and collectively the whole nation must maintain a central "bank", charging interest to maintain reserves against simultaneous runs on multiple banks. No device has ever been created for a nation to protect against a universal bank panic, which is as effective as placing the risk in the hands of private bankers who can expect to be stripped and shorn if things get out of control. Robert Morris demonstrated this point in 1779, and the nation seemingly must re-learn it every few decades. The IBM 360 computer made it possible to transform short-term into long-term in greater volume and lower cost by allowing banks to get bigger; but it could also perform the short-long transformation in cheaper ways than depository banks do, and from there the bank-competitive process we know as securitization has gone on to commercial credits, auto loans, credit cards, high-velocity stock trading, and mortgage-backed securities. These approaches are often cheaper and more convenient that the trusty old banking system, and Credit Default Swaps show its power isn't exhausted; any legislation to prohibit CDS is sure to to be circumvented. Insurance is also on the edge of being threatened. An industrial revolution of this magnitude takes decades of tweaks to become stabilized, but it will suffice for now, if we can establish reasonable protections against the risk shifted into the securitization or investment banking arena. As risk shifts, remuneration for accepting risk must shift as well. This new system for generating capital must not be starved because depository bankers resist the loss of their share of profitability; politics will have much to answer for if that happens.

Most likely, the main obstacles to getting this system fixed will come from overseas. Fifty years of disillusionment with the United Nations will make nations, the United States chief among them, resist loss of sovereignty in something so vital as finance. But that's for the future. For nearly a century, the past has been disrupted by idle notions of the fairness of coerced redistribution, in ways Mr. Wallison has succinctly described. But meanwhile we almost willfully ignore technological upheavals which everyone welcomed but no one fully anticipated.

http://www.philadelphia-reflections.com/blog/2049.htm

Planning Horizon: Review Benchmarks

S ome waggish but wise publication, perhaps *The Economist*, reported on the accuracy of predictions at various times in the future. Predicting what you can accomplish in a year is almost always an over-estimate; you can't possibly accomplish that much in a year. Predicting twenty years in advance has the opposite flaw; things will change so much in twenty years, the average person will almost invariably under-estimate the future. So, what's the best time for predictions? According to *The Economist*, it comes out to be about six years.

The Economist

Five years seems somehow easier to remember, so let's state a
principle of financial planning: review your goals every five years with some professional help. The young fellow needs to have a lawyer review his will, because he probably doesn't have one. He needs someone to take a hard and skeptical professional knife to the insurance salesmen who are currently circling their prey. And someone needs to review all of the government, tax and regulatory changes that will affect a young family. For most young people, the investment decisions about stocks and bonds are small because accumulations are small for everyone except professional athletes and entertainers.

If your investment pile is small enough, you can fool around a little. My father used to say the best thing that can happen to you is to lose some money when you are young. When you become tired of that, just make regular automatic deposits into a low-cost widely diversified no-load mutual fund that is very large, say, holding a trillion dollars in assets. It will pretty surely grow steadily in good times and bad, and serve as a warning benchmark for assessing all those fly-by-night investment managers who will besiege you when you accumulate enough money to be worth fleecing.

It's a pity to waste ten or so years of investment opportunity, however. Money at 7% will double in value every ten years. You will probably want to double your nest-egg as many times as you can, which is likely to have a ceiling at 10%, so figure doubling every seven years the rest of your life expectancy, and it is easily shown that frittering away those opportunities to double is a regular, pathetic, loss of opportunity for most of us between the age of sixteen and thirty. Take your hoped-for nest egg at retirement age and double it two and a half times, and you will see what a huge opportunity is regularly lost by just about everyone.

Your parents can improve on that by making investments on your behalf, starting the day you are born. That would cause five extra doublings of your investment accumulation at retirement. But plenty of people have learned the disappointments of betting on infant futures. If you can essentially afford to throw the money away as bad luck, go ahead and do it, but if you are risking someone's college education to do it, then you had better stay away.

A probably more serious debate can be generated by discussing the risks of giving money to teen-agers, who may then get all out of social control, throwing in your face, "It's my money and I'll do as I please". The main answer to that offensive discussion is to point out just what it is that most teenagers would do if they had the freedom to do it. Some frugal cultures like the Pennsylvania Dutch will give children some money, hide it secretly in a safe-deposit box without telling the child, and then reveal it when the child seems to be sensible enough to withstand the fever of a gold-rush. The worst outcome of all is to drain the incentives, depriving the child of reasons to work hard. Unfortunately, most teenagers now grow up in a suburb, where it is difficult to conceal the probable existence of assets.

http://www.philadelphia-reflections.com/blog/2127.htm

Locating Corporate Headquarters

The Right Angle Club was recently entertained by a director of the Greater Philadelphia movement, Troy Adams. One of their main purposes of spending several millions of dollars annually is to try to attract new businesses to Philadelphia. The money, interestingly enough, is contributed by other businesses, many of whom would be competitors of the newly attracted ones. What's the value of this? How do you go about doing it, even if it is a splendid idea?

Troy Adams

From the viewpoint of the city government, attracting new businesses means attracting new sources of taxation. It is not surprising therefore that the Chamber of Commerce tends to believe the main obstacle to attracting new business relocations is the tax structure of the locality. That's what the officers of companies under investigation ask about. By and large, the unattractiveness of Philadelphia to such inquiry is not the size of taxes, but their complexity. New businesses are turned off by learning of new types of taxes they had never heard of. It raises suspicion, and existing local businesses are quick to confirm that some of these strange-sounding taxes are objectionable mainly because you forget about them, and then get fined for not submitting a form to pay a small amount. If you get summoned to a hearing, it is even worse than paying the bloody thing. We have, say a lot of companies, branches in dozens of different cities, and we never heard of a tax like that. Of course, a famous sage once remarked that when someone complains it isn't the cost, it's the principle of the thing, well, it's the cost.

Chamber of Commerce

Regulations, requirements, prohibitions, deadlines, reporting requirements and all of that drive you crazy when you are trying to run a business. The cost of the taxes to a businessman is a simple question: do my competitors have to pay the same amount? If it's a level playing field, businesses ordinarily don't care about the money, since they can just raise the prices to the customer to cover it. Businesses, dear friends, don't look at costs the way the rest of us do. For that reason extended a little, businesses are strongly repelled by the existence of corruption, because corruption may or may not be applied equally, on a level playing field.

All of this sounded quite plausible to the Right Anglers, until Buck Scott spoke up. "I beg to disagree," he said. He remarked that in his experience the decision to move corporate headquarters to a city is determined by one person, or at most four. Whether the decision-maker is the CEO, a big stockholder, or a flunky assigned the task, the decision is usually not made on sensible economic grounds. It is based on the fact that the wife of the decision-maker grew up in Radnor or Chestnut Hill, and likes it here. If you are looking for access to ocean ports, railheads, Interstate Highways, airports, or proximity to big-city labor pools, Philadelphia has everybody beat. That sort of stuff is a given, and so what matters is that the decision maker wants to live here. To a certain extent, our proximity to New York and the District of Columbia is a handicap, since the lady of the family can live here while the corporate headquarters is not too far away, although too far away to be taxed. Buck Scott brought the discussion to a halt, because it was obvious to everyone that he had a strong point.

On another level, however, there is still debate. The question is whether Philadelphia gains a great deal by having the corporate headquarters located here. The CEO may have invisible value by his socializing frequently with the CEOs of other corporations, but no one was able to defend that as having serious advantages. Since the competitive corporations are paying for this effort to attract new corporate headquarters to the region, there may well be advantages to them which are not immediately evident. What's clearly of value is locating large numbers of employees to the region, since they do

Philadelphia Ports

generate business activity and hence taxes. Upscale companies have employees who are anxious to find good local schools, crime-free areas in which to live, and an improved environment; getting more of them into our voting pool will result in a better city, without question. Maybe, just maybe, locating the corporate headquarters in the region is a first step in enticing the rest of the company to come here. But it has not yet been demonstrated. Quite possibly, enticing the wives of decision makers to join the social whirl is the first step, and locating the factory here is only a secondary one which follows. Somehow, it begins to seem likely that the people who can influence one step, aren't talking to the people who determine the other.

http://www.philadelphia-reflections.com/blog/2063.htm

Corporations: Property, but also Immortal Persons

The Proprietorship of West Jersey is the oldest stockholder corporation in America. Devised by William Penn it has been doing business in Burlington, New Jersey since 1676. The Proprietorship of East Jersey may possibly have been created slightly earlier by William Penn, but recently dissolved itself, thus leaving a clear path for West Jersey to claim to be the oldest. For a hundred years before 1776, corporations were devised by the King through royal charters, and for a century after 1776 most state legislatures passed individual laws to create each corporation, one by one. Consequently, there were a great many variations in the powers and scope of older corporations, with heavy emphasis on the purpose to which the business was limited.

Proprietor House

Eventually, so many corporations were created that a body of law called the Uniform Law of Corporations simplified the task of incorporation for the legislatures. The Proprietorships of East and West Jersey would now probably be described as real estate investment trusts (REIT), but the Uniform laws now tend to diminish the emphasis on corporate purpose. It is now common to have a corporation proclaim the ability "to do whatever it is legal to do."

Lady Justice

Many voices have been raised in opposition to corporations, largely claiming unfairness for a large and established corporation to compete with newcomers, especially small newcomers striving for the same line of business. Because of its immortality, a stockholder corporation can achieve dominance no individual could hope for, while because of its multi-stockholder ownership, it can generally raise larger amounts of capital. Moreover, because of its size and durability a corporation can become more efficient and offer the public lower prices and higher quality. As much as anything else, a corporation can generally hire more employees and pay them higher wages; as even the unions admit, corporations create jobs, jobs, jobs. No doubt, state legislatures are attracted by the tax revenue derived from major corporations, but the quickest way to stimulate the economy has repeatedly been found to grow out of lowering corporation taxes. Since there is scarcely any purpose to creating a for-profit corporation unless it eventually pays its stockholders some kind of dividend, all corporation taxes have the handicap of double-taxation for a fixed amount of business. The Republic of Ireland recently lowered its corporate tax rate severely and triggered so much new corporate activity that it inflated and destabilized its whole economy. The result was a dangerous economic crisis, but politicians privately and world-wide silently derived only one real conclusion: lower your corporate taxes if you are looking to stimulate jobs, jobs, jobs.

The corporate model of business thus looks pretty safe, in spite of envious criticism, and is what most people mean when they speak of capitalism. The Constitution had the intention of extracting Interstate Commerce for the Federal Government and leaving the regulation of every other business to state legislatures. The Roosevelt Supreme Court-Packing dispute of 1936 twisted the meaning of Interstate Commerce to mean almost all commerce, but Congress wasted no time specifically exempting the "Business of Insurance" from federal regulation and returning it to the state legislatures in the 1945 McCarran-Fergusson Act. Although the matter remains one of some dispute, it is roughly correct to say that all commerce is federally regulated, except insurance. The corporation is nevertheless usually a creation of some legislature, and legislators have wide latitude in regulating them. To illustrate, in the early days of banking corporation, the Bank of Hartford was delayed in receiving incorporation by strong legislative suggestion that a closed stockholder list would result in refusal to incorporate them, whereas opening up the list to new stockholders might result in rapid approval. The implication was strong: the legislators wanted some cheap or free stock as a condition of incorporation. The following year, 250 banks were incorporated, and the year after that, over 400 more. Macing of incorporation applicants by politicians was sharpened to a fine point in Pennsylvania in the late 19th Century, when legislatures accorded monopoly status to public utility corporations, withholding it from competitors. It is now a textbook statement that the funding of substantially all municipal political machines is derived from voluntary contributions by utilities with politically granted monopolies, who are consequently indifferent to the retail prices of their products.

John Marshall

So there is still room for public concern and vigilance, and both the courts and the Constitution protect but restrain corporations. In the early 19th Century when public opinion was becoming firmer about incorporation, it was contended they should be treated as persons, possibly resembling real persons more closely by imposing a finite life span on their charters. Although corporation entities are still to some degree treated like individuals, the legal doctrine prevailed that they are in fact contracts between the state and the stockholders. The paradox is thus defended that although legislatures can create corporations, they cannot dissolve them! After all, a contract is an agreement between two parties, and it requires both parties to agree to dissolve the agreement. And then, the final uncertainty was removed by John Marshall. The U.S. Supreme Court in the

Dartmouth College case applied Article I, section 10 of the Constitution. That section provides that state governments may not pass any law impairing the obligation of contracts. The Supreme Court decision written by Marshall made it clear that this provision of Constitution eliminated any distinctiveness between a contract involving a state and a contract involving two citizens. There had been a growing feeling that private property was not to be disturbed by state power, and this linkage to Article 1 affirmed that point and finally settled matters. Shares of company stock were property, protected from state legislatures as belonging to the owner and not to the state in any sense. All the while that this quality of property was established, certain features of the corporation as a person endured. Most of the attention to this point arose after the Civil War, when the mixture of concepts (a slave was a person who was also private property) more or less applied to the institution of slavery as well. More recently, potential muddles have been created by limiting campaign contributions of corporations, thus impairing their right to free speech in the role of a person. It even appears to be true that some of the 1886 precedents were created by an error of a court reporter. The dominant precedent in operation here, would appear to a layman as, "If it ain't broke, don't fix it." Additional centuries including a Civil War thus encrusted conditions and traditions onto the hybrid idea of a corporation which now allow it to stand on its own feet, more or less free at last.

The legal profession can certainly be congratulated for constructing two institutions which include the majority of working Americans – the corporation and the civil service – without the slightest mention of either one in the Constitution. Although everything seems to be reasonably comfortable, and no one is actively proposing substitutes, it is uncomfortable to hear so much dissension about original intent of the Framers, when so much of American Law traces its history to events and institutions which the Framers never imagined. Constitutional Law, both within and without original intent, will soon be dwarfed in effect by non-constitutional accretions to it. Sooner or later, the advocates of some undefined cause could find it in their interest to challenge the Judicial system for what has been allowed to happen. Expediency has triumphed. We started with nothing but the common law (defined as law created by judicial decision), and we are slowly returning to that condition under a different name, misleadingly called statutes.

http://www.philadelphia-reflections.com/blog/2170.htm

Father of the Bureaucracy

Under the Articles of Confederation, America had a President who presided, but there was no executive branch for him to do anything administrative. The day to day business of the nation was conducted by committees of Congress, who mainly contracted out the actual work. Evidently, Robert Morris the businessman had observed this system with displeasure, because it only took him a few days to replace it with departmental employees, reporting to him. The affairs of the nation were evidently in such disarray that there is scarcely any recorded resistance to this astonishing re-arrangement, probably viewed as only one of a series of brisk actions by this foremost businessman of the nation, acting in an emergency and to some extent using his own money. Furthermore, the immediate administrative improvement was apparently so obvious to

Robert Morris

everyone that the system continued after Morris left office, and was absorbed into the 1787 Constitution without much recorded debate. Without dissent, as we say, the bureaucracy had been created. As the press of business steadily increased the bureaucracy, from a handful of employees to many millions of them, a fourth branch of government was created without any

Constitutional mission statement, not one single word. Following directions set by early America's preeminent no-nonsense businessman, control of the bureaucracy was placed within the Executive branch, in time largely located within the District of Columbia, and governed by rules made by the Civil Service Commission. Sometimes this fourth and largest branch of government skirts dangerously close to encouraging insubordination to their politically appointed superiors.

For some reason, the State Department is particularly suspected of such "Yes, Minister" behavior. Increasingly, government subcontractors are relied upon ("privatization"), as growth of public sector work forces a return to the subcontractor approach of two centuries earlier; such subcontractors increasingly find the bureaucracy assumes the role of a second Board of Directors. And for the same reason as before: the work of the central government keeps increasing. At a state and local level, an uncomfortable amount of political funding can be traced to utilities and other corporations who have been awarded legal monopolies, uncomfortably like the mercantilism which our colonist ancestors had found so repugnant to deal with. In the 21st Century we are finally approaching the point where we can foresee the number of people working for some level of government becoming greater than the number of voting citizens, and therefore able to control their income and the nature of their work. When the bureaucracy begins to exert political election power over its elected superiors, elected politicians are almost certain to rebel at what they will surely see as going a step too far. However, on the topic of salary and work environment, they are likely to become allies. Public discontent is already echoed in the growing political movement to limit or shrink the size of government; it would be well to examine and pilot test alternative options, before this one gets us into trouble.

In retrospect, this was one of many features of creating the three branches of government where broader implications went unnoticed in 1787. The British government had three branches, King, Parliament and Judiciary. To create a government consisting of a President, a Congress, and a Judiciary did not then seem like much of a departure. However, the Revolution deposed the King and made the people sovereign.

When the real implications of that breezy slogan had to be translated into legislative language serious implications emerged, unexpected then, and now hard to change.

http://www.philadelphia-reflections.com/blog/2168.htm

Power of the Purse

Liberty Bond

In 1917, Congress passed a law, quite possibly not understanding its full implications. From the founding of the republic until that time, Congress had approved the exact amount of each bond issue as enacted, neither more nor less. With the First Liberty Bond Act of 1917, however, Congress began to allow the administration to issue bonds as it pleased, up to some specified debt limit. Periodically since that time, as the amount in circulation approaches the debt limit, Congress raises the limit. No doubt this procedural change seemed like legislative streamlining, making it unnecessary for Congress to interrupt other activities to respond to a debt level which creeps up on its own time schedule. The overall effect of this change was significantly different however, and probably unintentionally.

If the authorized debt limit is raised by large enough steps, it effectively amounts to Congress turning over debt decisions to the executive branch. Conversely, raising the limit only a small amount soon triggers a repeat request, which by routine becomes so inconsequential that Congress stops paying attention to it.

Regardless of the size of the block grant, bulk authorization of blocks of debt results in the power of debt creation shifting toward the President. That was not what the Constitutional Convention intended.

Founding Fathers

The Founding Fathers remembered taxation as one of the main issues of the rebellion from England. Whether by King or President they had no intention of permitting the Executive to tax as he pleased; the issue traced back to the Magna Charta. Nor would they permit unlimited federal borrowing to generate escape hatches which would soon enough transform into higher taxes. Taxes therefore must originate in the House of Representatives, and bond issues were approved one by one. Following the 1917 liberalization it required only fifty years before unrestrained bond limits reached a point where future national debt obligations loomed beyond easy ability to pay them off. If they were ever pronounced unpayable by the international bond market, interest rates would rise, and eventually federal bonds would become unsalable. With Greece, Portugal and Ireland already flirting with bankruptcy, the approaching danger seems quite understandable to the voting public.

The issue is constrained by another barrier. The Fourteenth Amendment To the Constitution, Section Four, forbids dishonoring "the validity of the public debt of the United States, authorized by law." Enacted after the Civil War, this Amendment was intended to prevent future states or congresses from reversing the Reconstruction Acts, but it has the additional effect of preventing future Congresses from dishonoring interest and debt repayments on existing debt. The present Congress therefore retains

Constitutional Convention

the latitude to prohibit issuance of additional debt, but is forbidden from dishonoring existing debt.

This seems like a good principle to re-emphasize, entirely disregarding the merits of the TARP, the Dodd/Frank Act, or Obamacare. Indeed, restating the Constitutional intent for Congress to be chiefly responsible for taxes and debts, seems like a very good thing to do, quite regardless of whether present national debt limits ought to be raised. The 1917 Act was a mistake, probably an unconstitutional one, and should be reversed. Holding conferences in the White House about whether to issue debt raises uncertainty about whose duty it is. The responsibility belongs to the House of Representatives, and should stay there.

http://www.philadelphia-reflections.com/blog/2138.htm

Reviving Schuylkill: Eight Miles From the Dam to Ft. Mifflin

Joshua Nims of the Schuylkill River Development Corporation recently addressed the Right Angle Club about current activities of that organization. It's a non-profit corporation, but in a sense is a quasi-City agency, spending State and Federal funds, plus remediation funds. Just what remediation funds are was not clearly explained, but seem to be fines or assessments on companies who are thought to have fouled up the environment. Whether those assessments are fair or unfair, too small or too large, are political issues largely avoided in Mr. Nims' presentation, and hence are avoided here.

Joshua Nims

Gray's Ferry Bridge

The Gray's Ferry area is certainly an urban tragedy of epic proportion, but since its deterioration began in 1856, the events of the Civil War probably had a lot to do with it. Up until the Civil War, the western banks of the Schuylkill, especially around Gray's Ferry, were famously upscale and beautiful. The South Street Bridge, for example was originally envisioned as leading into a boulevard of the Arts, with the University Museum, Irvine Auditorium, the University Hospital and the mansions on the top of the hill setting off what promised to become a striking cultural statement. Anthony Drexel himself lived up there, walking it to work at Third and Chestnut. And that's just one famous example. It's hard to know what started the blight, but Harrison Brothers White Lead, Color and Chemical Works might be a good candidate, and the fact that the area soon developed the tracks of ten (10) smoke-belching railroads was certainly another major issue. The western bank of the Schuylkill rose to a high rocky promontory at Gray's Ferry, crowding wartime industrialization into a narrow place. Before that, Gray's Ferry Bridge had been the main artery to the South, traveled by George Washington many times, often stopping at Woodlands, that palatial home of Andrew Hamilton the original Philadelphia lawyer. A century before that, the Dutch fur traders had found it to be the first firm land after they sailed inland through the swamp, while the Indians knew it was the last forest area before you reached the (South Philadelphia) area of malaria, yellow fever and other mysterious vapors that must be avoided. In the sense of land travel, Gray's Ferry was therefore the most prominent part of the Philadelphia landscape for two centuries. The ferry itself was a floating bridge, pulled back and forth by ropes on each shore of the river. Given a choice of pretty much all of the North American continent, John Bartram placed his farm just south of this promontory. Where it still stands today, but surrounded by slums and urban decay.

Harrison Lead, Color
and Chemical Factory

It's a little hard to judge whether the Civil War pushed railroad construction into the only rocky crevice suitable, and then industrial pollution followed with vile and noxious effluents, or whether the Harrison Lead, Color and Chemical factory simply started it across the river in the riverbend. That's where the DuPont paint factory relocated in 1916, and in fact the Duponts get local blame as polluters when in fact they made considerable effort to clean things up after they acquired it. The area had a major slaughterhouse abattoir, and an asphalt plant, and several other major inducements to the populace to abandon their elegant mansions and run for their lives. The place now has old rusting bridges, tumble-down concrete pilings, lots of weeds, and not a single living fish for a century in that water. To diffuse the blame somewhat, it should be remembered that after the War of 1812, the Schuylkill was the main transportation artery for coal coming down from Pottsville and the rest of Schuylkill County. The river didn't have a sandy bottom, it was pulverized anthracite which releases acids and toxins when washed.

So that's the river region the Schuylkill Development Corporation plans to line with grassy running paths and benches to admire the view. Maybe the Wilson Steamship Line or something like it can again be persuaded to bring tourists here, or maybe the riverbanks can be lined with hotels to house people who take rides on river flatboats, as they do in San Antonio. Or dare we mention it, maybe Paris. Maybe Philadelphia can once again be a tax collector's idea of heaven, together with five-day weekends.

Schuylkill River
Development Corporation

At the moment, this little non-profit city agency is run on a $500,000 operating budget, and has about $20 million worth of projects in progress. Some of that is reparation money pried from the grand-children of the owners of those factories who did the damage over a century ago, and some large part of it is Philadelphia's share of the boodle from the Stimulus package. There's no doubt the area will look immensely improved in the next year or two, and a lot of hope that private investment will be attracted to an area previously shunned vigorously. The area which has already been cleaned up, from the Wissahickon to the Dam, really must be called a great success; there's lot's of foot traffic and joyousness. And the area can also be praised in what unfortunately is the measurement of modern urban development: it has only had two lawsuits for sprained ankles, and only two muggings, quite a commendable record. But now development is going past South Street, into much murkier areas, with more low-income residential spaces. Surveillance cameras are planned, and bright lighting, but it's far from certain that a little strip of gentrification can defeat miles of surrounding decay.

Only if they pull it off will private investment creep into the area, and the parents of University students permit their children to run there. If private investment arrives, this organization can do no wrong, because only then can it fairly be described as "Infrastructure". My own definition of infrastructure as an economic stimulus, is of early public spending on projects which would have eventually consumed the money anyway, except later. By that standard, infrastructure spending's only true cost would be the interest on borrowed money to do it sooner. Let's make a note to revisit this experiment in a couple of years, cautiously wishing everyone the best, in the meantime.

http://www.philadelphia-reflections.com/blog/2094.htm

Tyler Arboretum

There are over thirty arboreta in the Philadelphia region, and one of the oldest and largest is located in Delaware County. The 650 acres of the Tyler Arboretum, adjoining 2500 acres of state park, create a rather amazing wooded area quite close to heavily settled urban Philadelphia. The Arboretum is located on land directly deeded by William Penn, but it was privately held until 1940 and so is not as well known as several other arboreta of the region. The early Quakers, it may be recalled, often disapproved of music and "art work", so their diversions tended to concentrate on various forms of natural science. The first director of the Tyler, Dr. John Wister, planted over 1500

Tyler Arboretum

azalea bushes as soon as he took office in the 1940s. They are now seventy or eighty years old, quite old and big enough to make an impressive display. Even flowering bushes seemed a little fancy to the original Quakers.

The interests of the earlier owners of the property were more focused on trees, especially conifers. The property contains several varieties of redwoods, including one impressive California redwood said to be the largest east of the Mississippi. High above the ground it splits into two main branches, the result of a depredation by someone cutting the top off for a Christmas tree. So a large area near Painter Road is enclosed by a high iron fence, containing most of the conifer collection, and warding off the local white-tailed deer. Several colors of paint are to be seen high on many prominent trees, marking out several walking trails of varying levels of difficulty.

And then there are large plantings of milkweed, providing food for migrating butterflies; near a butterfly educational center. There are large wildflower patches and considerable recent flower plantings around the houses at the entrance. Because of the, well, Christmas tree problem, several houses on the property are still occupied.

The only serpentine barren in Delaware County is located on the property; we have described what that is all about in another essay. As you would imagine, there are great plant and flower auctions in the spring, conventions of butterfly and bird-watching groups at other times. The educational center is attracting large numbers of students of horticulture these days, and photographers. Flower gardens and photographers go together like Ike and Mike.

It's a great place for visitors, for members who are more involved, and for those with serious interests. With all that land to cover, some ardent walkers have enough ground to keep them regularly busy. Becoming a volunteer is a sign of serious interest, and that group is steadily growing. For a place that traces back to William Penn, it's slowly getting to be well known.

http://www.philadelphia-reflections.com/blog/2110.htm

Not a Single Red Knot

Horseshoe Crab

A full moon brings high tide, which for centuries has brought vast numbers of horseshoe crabs to the banks of the Delaware River, toward the end of May. Marine biologists tell us these ugly-looking beasts have evolved very little for thousands of years. Horseshoe crabs transport oxygen through their blood as a blue copper compound instead of that iron-containing hemoglobin the rest of us use. That's red, of course. Somewhere in the evolutionary path, these ancient animals also neglected to develop an immune system, but defend them-selves against bacteria by precipitating a sediment when they encounter endotoxin. By luck, this reaction takes place even though the bacteria are dead, so it is routinely employed as a way of detecting and eliminating endotoxin in intravenous fluids, which would otherwise go undetected by failing to grow the original bacteria in conventional culture media. Unfortunately, those of us who have never experienced a temperature spike to 106 degrees from an intravenous infusion of "sterile" water are more or less indifferent to the contribution of the Delaware crabs to our well-being. As well as being sadly indifferent to the unique nature of their nerve cells, in

Bombay Hook

long single neurons, which make a number of important experiments possible. The horseshoe crab offers still other attractions. When they come ashore to lay eggs (at full moon, or high tide, in May), they lay incredibly large quantities of them, attracting astonishing swarms of birds, which can be seen gliding a few feet above the water surface in groups of hundreds or even thousands. The Red Knot sandpiper is certainly not the only egg-eater at Bombay Hook, but there are some unique features of that bird to be mentioned in a minute. A lot of people object to being attacked by monster swarms of mosquitoes in the summer, but screens and air-conditioning have encouraged large number of rather prosperous houses to be built along the shore, particularly where there are sandy beaches. In fact, it is so crowded the Fish and Wild Life Service has placed street lights at such public places, with a narrow driveway to lead you to the beach. If you don't know how to recognize such amenities, well, too bad for outsiders.

The Red Knot

Although there are plenty of naturalists and bird-watchers who come in the early spring, most of the houses along "Slaughter Beach" seem to belong to fishermen and duck hunters, the two outdoor sports with most popularity. Different migrations of different food-producers bring different prey for the sportsmen, but somehow the most up-scale members of this fraternity tend to go there in May, looking for Red Knots. A Red Knot is a form of sandpiper, with a red head and breast. The birds are born in the Arctic tundra, eating vast amounts of mosquito eggs and larvae, migrating south in the fall. They winter over in Tierra del Fuego at the opposite end of the earth, and then migrate north to Bombay Hook on the Delaware. For these long migrations, they must eat voraciously when they do eat, and somehow have learned to look for the horseshoe crab eggs at just the right time, presumably following cycles of the moon for timing. Residents of the area for centuries have remarked on the timing of the birds and the tides and the crabs. Unfortunately, the two-continent migration was only recognized fairly recently, and when the supply seemed endless, the crabs were scooped up and used for fertilizer until their supply began to dwindle; both Delaware and New Jersey now have protective legislation, and Virginia is being verbally excoriated by bird watchers, to do the same. The crabs have started to come back, but the Red Knots are slower to respond; and now the threat is Sushi. Other ecological damage has reduced the supply of crabs in the Pacific, so the crab fishermen have migrated to the Atlantic to catch the crabs as bait for conch and other ingredients of Sushi. Once again, the abundance of crabs has declined, although to much smaller degree than the Red Knots. This year, on the very best day of the year for this sort of thing, with dozens of out-of-state license plates wandering aimlessly up and down thirty miles of shoreline, the shouted greetings among serious bird watchers returned the sad news, "No Red Knots today. Try xyz beach." It was generally agreed there was a bit too much wind for good Red Knot sighting, and that oil spills in the Gulf of Mexico were to be suspected, and that perhaps tomorrow would be a better day. But judging by the very expensive optical equipment these people were carrying around, these were serious birders, indeed. If they couldn't find Red Knots, the rest of us might as well give up.

The most plausible theory for the latest decline centers around the old-timer birds. When the first-timers start their northward migrations, they are guided by the old-timers who have made the trip at least once before. If something injures the flock, it may be a few years before the supply of old timers revives enough to supply the first-timers with guides. That's just a theory, of course, but currently the most popular one. Just what it would take to eliminate the

Red Knot migration completely, may now be close to being tested. Just on principle alone, it does seem a pity to eliminate a phenomenon which took thousands of years to develop.

When you finally give up on Red Knots, you might as well wander around this enormous wildlife sanctuary. A few miles up the road is the former location of Whitehall, the plantation house of Benjamin Chew, lawyer for the family of William Penn, and owner of the stone fortress

Benjamin Chew's Whitehall

on Germantown Avenue in Philadelphia that thwarted George Washington's attempt to stall and starve the British before they could join up with their ships in the harbor below Fort Mifflin. The original buildings on the plantation have disappeared, but the spongy plantation trails have been replaced by elevated gravel roads. So it is possible to roll up the windows of your car in mosquito season, turn on the air conditioning, and cruise around the spectacularly beautiful ponds and inlets. Further south is the plantation of Caesar Rodney, who rode to Philadelphia in the rain to cast the deciding vote for the Declaration of Independence. And further south of that is the plantation of John Dickinson, who made Rodney's ride necessary by refusing to sign the Declaration, on the grounds that the colonies showed insufficient unity, in his eyes, to be able to win a war with England. And anyway, the argument was largely economic, hence more likely to be won by economic means than military ones.

To the west of these historic plantations are some pretty impressive farms, new style. The houses give them away, since no farmer will spend a cent on his house if he can profitably expand his farm; these houses belong in glossy magazines. The silos are grouped in clusters of ten or twelve, the irrigation sprinklers are a quarter-mile long, attachable to what resembles a fire hydrant in the center of the field. There are over a hundred sheds on some farms, filled with chickens fattening up. And do you know what? You can drive for miles without seeing a single chicken.

Eventually, the road leads to the Dover Air Force Base, very large indeed. No planes are in evidence, as is true on most days. But one day in 1962 Mr. Kennedy was talking to Mr. Castro, and overhead at Dover you could see dozens, maybe hundreds, of eight-engine bombers. Just circling, circling, waiting for orders to go lay an egg on the Kremlin. It wasn't clear to onlookers at the time, just what this was all about. But the idea can now be entertained that perhaps Red Knots weren't the only species flirting with extinction.

http://www.philadelphia-reflections.com/blog/2141.htm

Black Swans (Financial Variety)

The mouth of the Delaware River once teemed with white swans, but black swans were unknown until the French explorer Nicolas Baudin brought home a few from Australia, where they are now celebrated as the state animal of Western Australia. The Empress Josephine Bonaparte was delighted with them, made them known as her birds, and thus made the term "Black Swan" more or less synonymous with rare chance occurrences. The implied inference that every white swan contains a remote potential for breeding a black one is doubtful biology, however. More likely, black swans are a distinct species – *Cygnus atratus* – confined to Australia and New Zealand, and just about extinct in New Zealand. In that view of things, the rarity of black swans is equivalent to the prevalence of

Nicholas Baudin

black ones, mixed within the population of generally white ones. Nevertheless, for this article it is convenient to continue the unlikely conjecture that most, or perhaps every, white swan contains a small potential to hatch a black one.

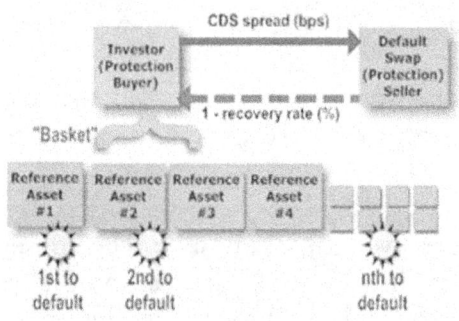

Credit Default Swaps

Many theories exist for the discovery that financial crises are commoner than chance alone would seem to predict; if they follow a Gaussian normal distri-bution curve, it must be somehow different from the distribution curve of smaller fluctuations. Observing this discordance is more or less how the phenomenon was discovered. The normal volatility of economic activity is calculated from the fluctuations observed in, say, twenty years. When that derived curve is extrapolated to include cataclysmic events which by theory of the unmeasured "long tail" occur every hundred years, speculators have later discovered by actual measurement that, alas, such disasters actually occur much more frequently. Calculated risks derived from such extrapolations have upended many insurance companies and insurance-like vehicles like Credit Default Swaps, who set their premium charges to match the mathematics. Since CDS approached a hundred trillion dollars in the last crisis, it is important to understand the mechanics of this kind of Black Swan if we possibly can.

One way to do that is to question the conventional equivalence of <u>risk and volatility;</u> that is, that the more markets bounce around, the riskier they become. Why should that be true, we might ask. And if it is somewhat true, why does that make its converse true, that calm seas are safe ones? Those of us who sit and watch the ocean shore soon adopt the habit of speech that high waves at the shore mean a storm is approaching, not that it will ever arrive. After all, the center of the storm may be traveling parallel to the coastline, not directly toward it. And calm seas are particularly undependable predictors; no matter how calm it may be, the next storm might

Black Swan

arrive in a few hours, or it may not come for months. Many other analogies spring up, once one puts aside the basic assumption that world economics can be depicted as a linear electrocardiogram. At the very least, they are two-dimensional, possibly three. Possibly four, if you regard time as a dimension.

It must be noticed that market volatility is universally viewed as linked to bad things, and many efforts have been made by central banks to reduce risk by constraining volatility. Alan Greenspan is famous for having controlled the economy for seventeen years without a major depression. Is that necessarily a good thing? Is it equally possible that kinetic energy was constrained within the inflating balloon until the bursting of it was a far more damaging explosion than small planned deflations would have been?

Experimental testing of these ideas has itself been constrained by an inability to predict the explosion point of expanding financial balloons. Planned deflations have been particularly feared, because of lack of assured ways to get them to stop deflating. But practical warnings such as these are not the same as claiming that lack of volatility is always the ideal state.

http://www.philadelphia-reflections.com/blog/2143.htm

Beaumarchais: A Playwright Brings France into the American Revolution

Pierre Augustin Beaumarchais, the son of an 18th Century French watchmaker, was born Protestant in a Catholic country. While possibly inclined by this circumstance to be a free thinker, his unusual artfulness was more likely inborn. After revolutionizing watchmaking before he reached the age of twenty, with an escapement mechanism for small portable watches, he rose to social attention when the Royal Watchmaker claimed the invention was his own, and Beaumarchais sued him. Thus gaining Louis XV's notice, Beaumarchais became Royal Watchmaker himself. He was soon giving harp lessons to the ladies of the court, writing plays like *The Barber of Seville*, and engaging in business schemes with wealthy investors. His career as a court favorite lasted sixteen years, first bringing him considerable wealth, but then sudden ruination by a lurid lawsuit

Pierre Augustin Beaumarchais

which cost him his fortune. In brief, Beaumarchais had tried to bribe a French judge with less money than his opponent offered, and so spent a few months in prison. After concluding a long, public battle through the appeals courts, he sought a more political role with the new young King, Louis XVI. He was sent to London to pay off a former French Agent, Chevalier D'Eon, who was blackmailing the French government. D'Eon's social connection to John Wilkes, the outspoken critic of the British King, sparked Beaumarchais' initial interest in Whig politics and the American rebellion cause.

John Wilkes

When he arrived in England Beaumarchais found British politics in turmoil; John Wilkes headed a whiggish opposition movement denouncing Royal authority and hosting gatherings of the like-minded, some of which Beaumarchais attended. Fueling these domestic British flames of liberal reform was the recent and increasingly serious rebellion on the other side of the Atlantic. As Beaumarchais spent more time in England discussing the rebellion with Virginian Arthur Lee (who highly exaggerated its strength), he became increasingly convinced it would be a good strategy for France to help the colonists. For all the trouble Arthur Lee ended up causing, he can fairly claim credit for enlisting Beaumarchais to French support for the American Beaumarchais reported his findings to Charles Gravier, Comte de Vergennes, the foreign minister of France. He urged the French government to support the American rebellion, consistently taking the line of French self- interest; after suffering a humiliating defeat in the Seven Year War, France might now undermine England's growing regional power by helping the colonists loosen their affiliation to the rising island empire.

When the young and hesitant Louis XVI finally agreed to take Beaumarchais' advice, it was still unclear whether the American rebellion was a serious movement. The French monarchy was not ready to unsettle its already shaky relationship with England by coming out in public support of untested rebels. To preserve the appearance of neutrality, the French Government loaned Beaumarchais one million livres in June 1776 to start a private trading firm, the Roderiguez Hortales Company. This new firm would buy old French military supplies from the French government, then re-sell those supplies to the Americans with return payment of American products, primarily tobacco.

Charles Gravier, Comte de Vergennes

Beaumarchais was therefore expected to run a completely self-sustaining operation, free from association with the French government. Rogue and adventurer that he was, Beaumarchais took on this risky challenge with enthusiasm, working tirelessly in France and around Europe to provide the Americans with ammunition, military supplies and food. His efforts did not go undetected, however. England's ambassador to France, Lord Stormont, grew suspicious of Beaumarchais' frequent trips across the channel and notified the French government of his displeasure. But Beaumarchais simply ignored these protestations.

Louis XVI

Matching Beaumarchais' work in establishing Rodrigez and Hortalez, the American Congress sent a covert representative to nurture French support. Silas Deane, sent to France under the disguise of a colonial merchant in July 1776, learned of Beaumarchais' plan to support the American army and at first the two became fast friends. Unfortunately this friendship sparked the jealousies of Colonists and Frenchmen alike. Arthur Lee became a particularly vicious opponent of the Beaumarchais/Deane pair, resenting Silas Deane for having been chosen over him as diplomat to the French, and suspecting Beaumarchais of money laundering. Even when he was later sent in company with Benjamin Franklin to continue negotiations with France, Lee remained suspicious of Deane and Beaumarchais' collaboration. The American mission to France during this period remains famous for strife and factionalism, which was as much a free for all as two-sided animosity. Personal ambition and cultural differences complicated these relationships; no one eventually suffered more because of it than Beaumarchais and Deane.

While Deane negotiated with Beaumarchais, Arthur Lee corresponded with Congress to undermine both Beaumarchais and Silas Deane. Lee was highly suspicious of both men, accusing them of using the privateering scheme for their own profit. The result was a split in Congress between those who supported Lee and those who supported Deane's work with Beaumarchais. The first congress was full of alliances, tempers and faulty information that led to frequent, if not constant, conflict. The Lee brothers were particularly vocal opponents of an alliance with France, and this opposition by a prominent family within the Continental Congress kept French and American relations strained and hesitant.

Silas Dean

The first shipment to the colonies by the Rodrigez and Hortalez Company carrying nearly 25,000 pounds of ammunition, was a shaky and often blind operation. Continental Congress never received news of Deane's plans (and request for ships) and remained busy working away at a proposed Declaration of Independence, the publication of which would, with luck, ensure France's official cooperation. Deane was forced to make crucial shipment decisions without the support or approval of Congress. Adding to this instability, the ships were discovered by Lord Stormount right before the first shipment left for the colonies, and the English Ambassador to France quickly protested their sailing to the French government. Vergennes, eager to keep smooth relations with England, particularly in view of the seeming failure of the American cause at that time, officially banned their sailing off the French coast. Fortunately for the Americans, Beaumarchais sent the supplies anyway, which were greeted

Barber of Seville

warmly by colonists in Portsmouth, New Hampshire in early 1777. These supplies helped the colonists win the Battle of Saratoga, the success of which finally convinced the French to emerge in full support of the American Revolution. Beaumarchais continued to supply the Colonists despite England's protests, but privateering increased the threat of war between England and France.

By September 1777, Beaumarchais had shipped 5 million livres worth of supplies to America without repayment. By 1778 his firm had accrued so much debt that by the end of the war it was in complete ruin. The French government was unwilling to acknowledge its support for Beaumarchais before or after the war, and Silas

Deane's entreaties were, unfortunately, not enough to convince Congress that the American colonies owed Beaumarchais for his generous work. Beaumarchais continued his requests for compensation after the war, and Congress continually refused or ignored these requests. Thirty six years after his death, his heirs were paid back a small fraction of the original debt. Forced to travel to congress to fight their ancestor's case, his descendants were awarded 800,000 livres of the several million owed. In effect Beaumarchais nearly single -handedly supplied the American Revolution with arms receiving very little in return except his financial ruin.

It is surprising that a man with so much talent and character should have died in near obscurity; yet Beaumarchais' plays, not his political maneuverings, are what have survived today as part of the standard repertory. When his wildly successful *The Barber of Seville* premiered in 1775, Beaumarchais was already a well-known playwright and champion of the down-trodden common man. Perhaps he was too great for his own time; *The Barber* proved more popular when adapted into a libretto by Lorenzo Da Ponte and then later into an opera by Gioachino Rossini in 1814. An independent mind and flamboyant character immortalized his art, but the same characteristics may have brought him, and France, to political and financial ruin.

http://www.philadelphia-reflections.com/blog/2125.htm

Christmas, 1776, Behind the Scenes at Trenton

Cornwallis and the British regulars came thundering down the narrow waist of New Jersey from New Brunswick to Trenton, just before Christmas, 1776. Washington's troops retreated before them, fleeing to the Pennsylvania side of the Delaware River. The British then fortified the Hessians in Trenton and went back into their own winter quarters nearer New York. Plenty of time seemed available to finish off Washington in the Spring, and then leisurely conquer the enemy's capital in Philadelphia. The Continental Congress

Washington Crossing the Delaware

thought so, too, and moved its capital to Baltimore. Only three members of the Congress, Robert Morris, George Clymer, and George Walton (of Georgia), remained in Philadelphia to run the government; Morris was essentially in charge, in the role of financier whatever that meant. With Congress seeking refuge, Morris was for practical purposes, acting President of the United States. Washington swept up all of the boats on the Delaware, set up camp on the Pennsylvania side, and begged Morris to get him some money to reward re-enlistments by January 1. Others saw the end of the year as Christmas time; Washington saw it as the end of the year when enlistments expired. He quite plainly stated that it was all over for the Continental Army unless he could get some hard currency, silver preferred, to show the troops that the rebellion could survive another year. About ten dollars per soldier would probably do it, but then there was also a need for hard money to buy food and supplies for the starving troops.

General Charles Cornwallis

Just how Morris managed to find the money is unclear, or how much of it was his own. But he did manage, with the lucky arrival of a gunpowder smuggling ship from France, and eighteen cannon somehow supplied by General Knox. The Colonials rallied to re-cross the Delaware, surprise the Hessians, outmaneuver Cornwallis as he once more thundered back down the New Jersey waist, now intent to wreak vengeance. The military essence of it all reached a climactic moment when Washington used fake bonfires to trick the British while he sneaked around them. Captain Sam Morris and Philadelphia's First City Troop managed the bonfire deception. When cannon fire in Princeton announced the trick, the British raced back to their ships at Staten Island to protect their supplies before Washington who now had a head start, could get to the ships, leaving the British to starve in the woods. Both sides were exhausted by the chase, and although he had won this race, Washington had to retreat to winter quarters in Morristown, New Jersey (named after a former New Jersey Governor.) Meanwhile with Congress taking refuge in Baltimore, Philadelphia was nearly deserted except for some Quakers who felt they had no quarrel with the British. And Robert Morris, who continued to run his smuggling operation with Beaumarchais the famous playwright on the French end of it. Tradition has it that some Quaker gardens were dug up to find enough silver to reward reenlistments, and if so it is unclear how much was freely contributed and how much was just plain stolen; indeed, how much of it might have been Morris' own money. By the next fall, Washington was able to fight the largest battle of the war at the Brandywine Creek, so Morris must have been very active smuggling guns and gunpowder to resupply the Colonials during that intervening winter and spring.

During periods of lull in infantry warfare, other warfare including privateering at sea, blockades, and the diplomatic intrigue in Paris, were unmerciful. If Washington's army had been wiped out, the Revolution would have ended. But other misadventures might have ended it as well. The colonists were demoralized, and their dismay was summarized by a letter from Morris to Silas Deane, a line of which was the bitter observation that, "Sorry I am to say it, many of those who were foremost in noise, shrink coward-like from the danger.".

A few days before that fateful Christmas, Ben Franklin had arrived in Paris to take over our diplomatic mission with the French. When the news of Washington's victory reached him, the new American arrival was being acclaimed as the world-famous scientist and witty author, and was thus in a position to make the most of it with the French court. He may be forgiven for exaggerating Washington's exploits a little. The Trenton victory was rough and ragged, but it would serve. Washington, Franklin, and Morris. The three Americans who mainly won the Revolutionary War for us now took the stage, front and center.

http://www.philadelphia-reflections.com/blog/2117.htm

Battle of Monmouth

A moving army tends to get strung out on roads through unfamiliar territory, and when boarding ships leaves a steadily diminishing rear guard to protect the fleet. Thus, General Clinton's retreating British army presented an opportunity for Washington to harass them, take advantage of unexpected delays, and to be wherever they were going. So Washington ordered the Continental Army out of Valley Forge, to pursue the retreating British as they moved over the Delaware River to Camden, joining the King's Highway at Haddonfield, heading for Sandy Hook and the waiting ships of the British Navy. As both armies approached Monmouth Court House, Washington caught up with Clinton and ordered his deputy, General Charles Lee, to attack with an advance force that would hold the British in place until Washington's main force could catch up. Both armies had about 13,000 soldiers in strength, but only 9,000 of Clinton's men were engaged because of their strung-out deployment.

Battle of Monmouth

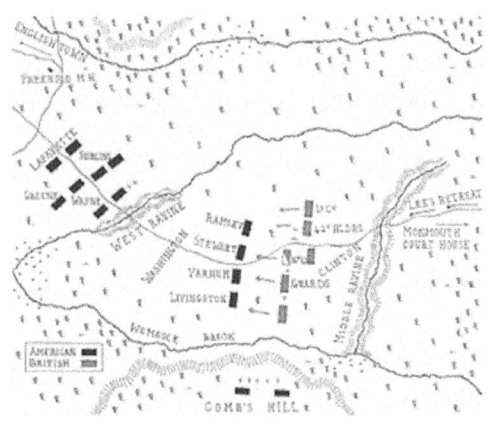
Battle of Monmouth map

Washington's battle plan was therefore vindicated, and he next showed his characteristic ability to use terrain to his advantage. The New Jersey countryside breaks up into hills as it approaches New York harbor, and its valleys between hills tend to contain creeks at the bottom. Therefore, the retreating British were forced into narrowing valleys which exposed them to flanking maneuvers, but reduced the room for Washington to be outflanked. Lee failed to take such effective advantage of the terrain and made only half-hearted attacks; when Washington and the main body of troops caught up with him, Lee was promptly relieved of command and later court-marshaled. In his place, Washington sent Nathaniel Greene around the enemy's southern flank, setting up four artillery pieces on a high hill, protected from British attack by a flooded creek. He was thus able to *enfilade* the British line, aiming cannon balls at the near end where they would bounce up the British line if they fell short, or land in the far end of the British line when they overshot. The cannons now look fairly small and puny, but with a well-trained crew of a dozen artillerymen each one could get off five to ten shots a minute. With four pieces of artillery they could drop twenty to forty shots a minute onto the confused and compressed formation of enemy troops. The battle went on all day, the longest battle of the Revolution.

Under the cover of darkness, Clinton withdrew his troops toward Sandy Hook, leaving six hundred casualties on the ground, two thirds of them British. The British could claim they achieved their objective of reaching the ships, but with greater casualties, and forced to withdraw in the face of discovering a much better-disciplined American army than they had ever faced. They acquired new respect for Washington, who demonstrated boldness and outstanding tactics, with a professionalism quite equal to their own.

http://www.philadelphia-reflections.com/blog/2149.htm

Pennsylvania: Browbeaten Into Joining a War

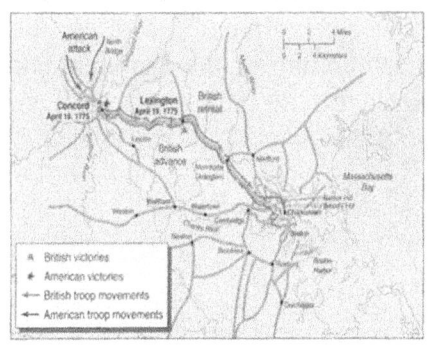

Battle of Lexington

In April, 1775, colonial militia were shooting it out with British soldiers at Bunker Hill and Lexington/Concord. If you include the December 16, 1773 Boston Tea Party, Massachusetts had been fighting the British for almost three years before July 4, 1776. It had never been absolutely clear to Pennsylvanians just what they were fighting about in New England, beyond the fact that a considerable store of gunpowder was hidden in Lexington and Concord and British soldiers had been sent to confiscate it, along with those two trouble-makers, Samuel Adams and John Hancock. The militiamen behind the trees were just as British as the soldiers were, and their short slogan of fair treatment was to elect representatives to any Parliament which claimed a right to tax them. Snubbed by a high-handed King, they got his attention by shooting back when the King tried to enforce laws they had not had a chance to vote on. Seeing your neighbors shot soon clarifies your options. Other colonies, especially Pennsylvania, Delaware and South Carolina, were slower to anger about either taxation or representation, worrying more about the motives of unstable leaders in Massachusetts like Samuel Adams, and content to stall while British Whigs led by Edmund Burke and the Marquess of Rockingham tried to civilize the king's ministry. Besides, the British were not attacking Pennsylvania.

To be fair to the hot-headed New Englanders who were apparently stirring up so much unprovoked trouble, a better case could have been made against the heedless British ministry, and New England lawyers should have made it. Following the Boston Massacre, there was genuine alarm among lawyers like John Adams that King George was eroding historic legal rights achieved over several centuries, indeed, preferentially undermining them more for mere colonists than for U.K. citizens with a vote. The Navigation Acts of the British government in particular were offensive to American colonists; randomly chosen representatives on juries proceeded to render them unenforceable with a wide-spread refusal to convict. They were employing William Penn's strategy of "Jury Nullification", and better acknowledgment of its legal history was sure to make a favorable impact on Philadelphia minds. Somehow, the Boston legal community felt this line of argument was too specialized to be effective, or else shared the alarm of their enemy the British Ministry that Jury Nullification in the hands of public could be too hard to control. John Adams had made a particularly famous defense of John Hancock who was being punished with confiscation of his ship and a fine of triple the cargo's value.

Adams was later singled out as the only named American rebel the British refused to exempt from hanging if they caught him. As everyone knows, Hancock was the first to step up and sign the Declaration of Independence, because by 1776 there was also widespread colonial outrage over the British stratagem of transferring cases to the (non-jury) Admiralty Court. Many colonists who privately regarded Hancock as a smuggler were roused to rebellion by the British government thus denying a defendant his right to a jury trial, especially by a jury almost certain not to convict him. To taxation without representation was added the obscenity of enforcement without due process. John Jay, the first Chief Justice of the Supreme Court of the newly created United States, ruled in 1794 that "The Jury has the right to determine the law as well as the facts." And Thomas Jefferson built a whole political party on the right of common people to overturn their government, somewhat softening it is true when he saw where the French Revolution was going. Jury Nullification then lay fairly dormant for fifty years. But since the founding of the Republic and the reputation of many of the most prominent founders was based on it, there may have seemed little need for emphasis of an argument any modern politician would seize with glee.

Bunker Hill

At that time, only a third of colonists were in favor of fighting about it, and a third were entirely opposed. Samuel Adams himself had written his supporters that it would be best to hold back until greater revolutionary support could be gathered. Unfortunately, in the minds of the British ministry, hostility had already escalated irrevocably when the Continental Congress in June 1775 created the Continental Army and dispatched George Washington to Boston to join the fight. This was probably the moment when war became inevitable in the collective mind of the British Parliament; a full year had passed since then. Regardless of Bunker Hill, the British were incensed by the creation of the Continental Army, and passed the Prohibitory Act, which declared that all thirteen colonies (belonging to the Congress) were renegades, their decision to raise armies placing them "outside the protection of the king". All American shipping was now subject to seizure, not just that of Massachusetts, as were foreign vessels engaged in American trade. News of this Parliamentary thunderbolt first came to Robert Morris through one of his ships, accompanied by news that 26,000 troops had been raised for an invasion of American ports. The British position was that all thirteen colonies had gratuitously formed a government and an army, and needed to be punished for such treason. Pennsylvania was no exception; the offending Continental Congress had met there, and Benjamin Franklin had represented both Massachusetts and Pennsylvania before Parliament. Confirmation of that particular British attitude toward them greeted Pennsylvanians when British warships promptly appeared in May 1776, to patrol the mouth of the Delaware. Three cruisers exploring up the river were attacked by American galleys. In response, the cruisers sailed directly at Philadelphia until they were finally beaten back by citizen flotillas, supervised by Robert Morris and the Committee on Safety. Morris wrote to

Silas Deane in Paris that war was probably inevitable. Far less tentatively, the British felt it had already been in progress for a year.

The British Ministry had probably been unreasonably hostile, but they were not unanimous and they were not fools. In response to colonial unrest up until these almost irretrievable events, the British were concentrating on depriving the colonists of arms and gunpowder, mostly avoiding direct violence; it seemed an effective strategy. During the Boston Tea Party, for example, British warships in Boston harbor merely stood by and watched the fun. Although gunpowder was a simple chemical, comparatively easy to make, it was less likely to blow up in your face if finely ground and milled in a major factory; for a real Colonial war it had to be imported. The British strategy had been: Take away their weapons, and they will capitulate. Unfortunately that was not the response at all, since even loyal colonists felt they needed good gunpowder for hunting and self- protection. Gunpowder blockades and confiscations were going to be bitterly resented. Nevertheless, British patience with the colonists was probably only irretrievably exhausted in June, 1775, when the Continental Congress formed its own army and Washington marched them to Boston. If Pennsylvania became convinced of that inevitability, the war was certainly on. After the naval battles right here on the Delaware, what really became hard to believe was that – only a week earlier – Pennsylvania's moderate voters had soundly defeated the revolutionary radicals in an Assembly election.

Pennsylvania had indeed been far less eager to fight than Massachusetts and Virginia, but the more belligerent colonies felt they needed allies in order to prevail. In the Continental Congress Pennsylvania and South Carolina voted against rebellion in the Spring of 1776; and in the May 1776 election where independence was the main issue, the Pennsylvania voters elected an Assembly 70% opposed to rebellion, including that eminent merchant Robert Morris. Some of the determined Massachusetts efforts to persuade the Mid- Atlantic colonies bordered on subversion, but Pennsylvania remained unmoved. Nevertheless, they could see a real danger of war, and had approved Secret Committees to be prepared if it came. Robert Morris was ideal for covert activity and could be expected to keep the activity under control, along with Benjamin Franklin and several prominent merchants. Morris made no secret of his affection for England the country of his birth, or of his membership in the John Dickinson group which hoped economic pressures would suffice. When the Secret Committee chairman suddenly died of smallpox, Morris was then appointed chairman. His personal integrity was widely respected; in several hotly contested elections, he was nominated by both the radicals and the conservatives.

> *"It seems absolutely necessary to prepare a vigorous defense, since every account we receive from England threatens nothing but destruction."*
>
> **Robert Morris**
> **December 1775**

> *"For my part I abhor the name & idea of a rebel, I neither want or wish a change of King or Constitution & do not conceive myself to act against either when I join America in defense of Constitutional Liberty."*
>
> **Robert Morris**
> **December 1775**

The Secret Committee was charged with smuggling in some gunpowder, just in case. Several of the members agreed to ship arms and gunpowder in their own ships; there was no one else to do it. The decision to engage in treasonous gunrunning was greatly assisted by the unexpected appearance of two Frenchmen with aristocratic accents in a boat loaded with gunpowder, who proposed themselves as French counterparties in a major gunpowder and weapons smuggling network which did actually materialize. Just who sent them has never been made entirely clear, but later events make the playwright Beaumarchais a reasonable guess, acting as a secret agent of the French King. Beaumarchais the famous playwright had been caught in a police trap, and forced to act as a government spy; just whose agent he was is a little murky. The American merchants on the Secret Committee knew gun running was expensive for them; they all expected to be paid for dangerous work, so it was also profitable. And treasonous. If caught, there was every possibility of being hanged. Initially, the Americans all imagined the Frenchmen were simply in it for the money, and that is possible. Surprisingly, no one seems even to have speculated they were agents of the French government on a mission to stir up trouble against the English. Spies had surely informed the French King of approaching war, at least six months before the Americans knew of it. Since these two foreign shippers (giving their names as Pierre Penet and Emmanuel de Pliarne, and surely sent to spy) demanded to be paid in hard currency, Morris did send one ship with hard money to pay for munitions to be carried in its hold on the return voyage. But he soon devised safer payment approaches.

Since he had agents and offices in most major foreign ports, Morris could arrange for the money to arrive independently of the cargo ships. Or better yet, send ordinary commodities on the outward journey and make a private profit on that, returning with munitions paid for by the "remittances" – revenue from the other cargo. Money was also sent on other circuitous journeys and through other channels, particularly the discounted debt system he had earlier perfected when paper currency had been prohibited. There was thus less incriminating evidence on the ship, and even if the ship burned or everyone got hanged, the money was at least out of the hands of the enemy. Secrecy was of course essential, this activity could be called treasonous, and it was most assuredly smuggling. When neutral countries were found supporting gunrunning, that assistance might well be called an act of war, so all nations prohibited it. In spite of his earlier reluctance about independence, Morris could easily see that gunrunning by the privateers of a recognized nation might be better protected by the conventions of war than exactly the same activity conducted by, say, brigands, profiteers or pirates.

Gunrunning was always seriously dangerous; Morris soon lost four ships, one by a mutiny of secretly loyalist sailors, and two were captured by unscrupulous American privateers. There would be some protection from hanging for gun runners as authorized combatants of a recognized nation. In retrospect we can now surmise that Franklin was committed to independence, and was probably nudging his friend on the Secret Committee.   John   Adams could barely contain himself, openly and repeatedly. Washington was already outside Boston leading an army. Commitment had many levels.

In July, 1776 Morris was called on to vote in Congress for the independence he always said he opposed. Caesar Rodney rode in from Delaware to deliver his state for Independence; now, Pennsylvania alone stood in the way. When the moment came, on the advice of Franklin, Robert Morris and John Dickinson left the room to allow other Pennsylvania delegates to constitute a Pennsylvania majority, casting the state's vote for the war. Commitment to the war had many variants, even after the war began.

http://www.philadelphia-reflections.com/blog/2113.htm

Fort Wilson

October 4, 1779. The British had conquered but abandoned Philadelphia; order was still only partially restored. Joseph Reed was President of the Continental Congress, inflation ("Not worth a Continental") was rampant, and food shortages were at near-famine levels because of self-defeating price controls. In a world turned upside down, Charles Willson Peale the painter was leader of a radical group of admirers of Rousseau the French anarchist, called the Constitutionalist Party, leaners in the radical direction actually followed by the French Revolution in 1789. Peale was quick to admit he had no clue what to do with his leadership position, and soon resigned it in favor of painting portraits of the wealthy. Others had deserted the occupied city, and many had not yet returned. The Quakers of the city hunkered down, more or less adhering to earlier instruction from the London Yearly Meeting to stay away from any politics involving war taxes. About two hundred militia roamed the city

James Wilson

streets making trouble for anyone they could plausibly blame for the breakdown of civil order. Philadelphia was as close to anarchy as it would ever become; the focus of anger was against the pacifist Quakers, the rich merchants, and James Wilson the lawyer.

Fort Wilson

Wilson had enraged the mob by defending Tories in court, much as John Adams got in trouble for defending British troops involved in the Boston Massacre; Ben Franklin advised Wilson to leave town. It is still possible to walk the full extent of the battle of Fort Wilson in a few minutes, and a pity the tourist bureau has not marked it out. Begin with the Quaker Meeting at Fourth and Arch. A few wandering militiamen caught Jonathan Drinker, Thomas Story, Buckridge Sims, and Matthew Johns emerging from the Quaker church, and rounded them up as prisoners. The Quakers were marched down the street for uncertain purposes when the militia encountered a group of prominent merchants emerging from the City Tavern. Unlike the meek Quakers, Robert Morris and John Cadwalader the leader of the City Troop ordered the militia to release the prisoners, behave themselves, and disperse; Timothy Matlack shouted orders. It was exactly the wrong stance to take, and about thirty prominent citizens were soon driven to retreat to the large brick house of James Wilson, at the corner of Third and Walnut, known forever afterward as Fort Wilson. Doors were barred, windows manned, and Fort Wilson was soon surrounded by an armed, shouting, mob. Lieutenant Robert Campbell leaned out a third story window, and was soon dropped dead by a lucky bullet. Crowbars were sought, the back door forced open, but the angry mob immediately scattered after fusillades from inside.

Down the street came President Reed on horseback, ordering the militia to disperse, with Timothy Matlack at his side; both men were well-known radicals, switching sides to maintain law and order. The City Troop arrived, an order was given the cavalry to Assault Every Armed Man. The mob was finally dispersed by this makeshift cavalry charge, cutting and slashing its way through the dazed militia. When it was over, five defenders were dead and about twenty wounded. Among the militia the casualties were heavier, but inaccurately reported. Robert Morris took James Wilson in hand and retreated to his mansion at Lemon Hill; Wilson was the founder of America's first law school. Among other defenders huddled in Fort Wilson were some of the future signers of the Constitution from Pennsylvania: General Thomas Mifflin, Wilson, Morris, George Clymer. Equally important was the deep impression left on radical leaders

Joseph Reed

like Reed and Matlack, and Henry Laurens, who could see how close the whole war effort was to dissolution, for lack of firm contol. Inflation continued but the conter-productive price control system was abandoned and never revived; the patriots had a bad scare, and the heedless radicals forced to confront the potentially disastrous consequences of their own amateur performance when entrusted with the power and responsibility they had just been demanding. It was one of those rare moments in a nation's history when the way suddenly opens to previously unthinkable actions.

Timothy Matlack

The Battle of Fort Wilson was the only Revolutionary War battle fought within Philadelphia city limits; a revolution within a revolution, every participant was a Rebel patriot. Reed and Matlack were the two most visibly appalled by the whole uproar, forced by circumstances to attack the forces of their own political persuasion. But it seems very certain that Robert Morris and the other prosperous idealists were also left with an indelible conviction that even a confederation must maintain central command and discipline with an iron will, or all might be lost. A knowledgeable French observer estimated that Robert Morris then owned assets worth eight million dollars, an almost unimaginable sum for the time. But he would lose every penny if effective political control could not be restored. A few days later in the October election, he and all the other

Republican (conservative) officials lost their seats. It did not matter; Morris then knew what to do and his opposition didn't.

http://www.philadelphia- reflections.com/blog/2144.htm

Fort Washington, PA

The Revolutionary War lasted eight years, so there are a half dozen Fort Washingtons, in several states. Pennsylvania's Fort Washington gets free advertising from being a stop on the Pennsylvania Turnpike at the intersection of the East-West branch and the North-South branch, near some very large shopping malls. Nevertheless, the suburbs haven't reached it yet, and it is on a series of wooded mountain ridges discouraging housing development. Another way of describing its location is that it is several miles north of Chestnut Hill along the Bethlehem Pike, a road which begins in the center of Chestnut Hill at Germantown Avenue. The Pike is quite old, with many surviving colonial-era houses and inns to liven up the trip.

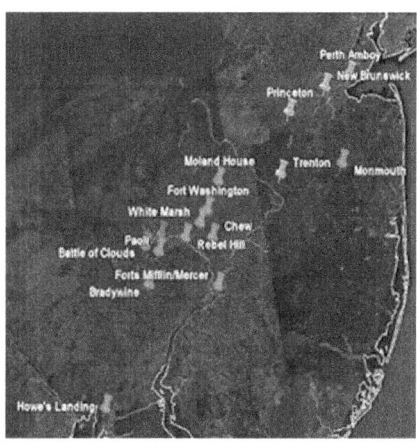

British Campaigns, 1777 - 1778

A third way to describe Fort Washington is that the headquarters were at the point where Bethlehem Pike crosses the Wissahickon Creek. How's that again? How does the western Wissahickon Creek then flow uphill to Chestnut Hill? Of course, it doesn't, but the appearance takes some explaining. The northwestern end of Philadelphia is reached by two ancient roads running on ridges quite close together like the split tail of a fish. Germantown Avenue runs up one ridge, and Ridge Avenue runs up the second ridge closer to the Schuylkill. The Wissahickon runs in the gully between these two ridges, and tumbles down the hill at Wissahickon Avenue, or Rittenhousetown if that is more understandable. The ridge of Ridge Avenue is essentially cut off by the creek, but engineers have put Ridge Avenue on a high arching bridge as it crosses the creek far below, and by this magic Ridge Avenue and Germantown Avenue are at about the same height most of the way. The Wissahickon Creek is really running downhill the whole way, but sort of disappears from sight and reappears as it twists through the gorges, misleading the casual visitor (or commuter). As happened so often during the Revolutionary War, Washington showed his understanding here of geography in the service of guerrilla warfare.

Since the British were headquartered in Germantown, and the Americans were camped a few miles away on the same creek, it was inevitable there would be some sort of battle in the region. Washington launched a three-pronged attack on the British soon after arriving at Fort Washington, but his troops fired at each other in the fog, and apparently two prongs more or less got lost in the gorges. The Americans retreated, and the British consolidated their conquest of Philadelphia. They did launch one surprise attack on the American encampment (the Battle of Whitemarsh), but that was mainly a reconnoiter, given up after a few days when it became clear Washington's troops held the high ground. It really is high ground (hawk-watching platforms and all) for reasons already stated. Chestnut Hill is a pinnacle sticking up on the west side of the Creek, with the Wissahickon snaking around its base.

This really was a perfect place for Washington to aim for after the Brandywine Battle, close enough to threaten the British, located in a bowl-like valley for camping, but terminating at the top of a mountain ridge in case the British counter- attacked. And with plenty of running water from the Wissahickon. However, it was a little too close for comfort, and he withdrew across the Schuylkill into Valley Forge as a more substantial natural fortress. Valley Forge is also on a hilltop, but one sitting in the middle of the Great Valley (Route 202 to Wilmington), like the center of an angelfood cake tin. No doubt, the advantages of this new location became evident to him at the earlier skirmishes of the Battle of the Clouds, and the Paoli Massacre, which occurred nearby.

In retrospect, these maneuvers and skirmishes were of little military significance, except for the major Battle of Brandywine. The lost opportunity was the chance to catch the British Army without supplies or access to the Navy, aborted by what was probably a hurricaine, the so-called Battle of the Clouds. Philadelphia was lost, and the opportunity to win the war early by smashing a third British army, was gone for good. The defeat of the Hessians at Trenton, the loss of Burgoyne's army at Saratoga, and a victory on the outskirts of Philadelphia might together just have finished the War. But things didn't work out, the British similarly missed some opportunities, and the war was to last another five years. Once the French allied themselves, their wealth and naval strength tended to make French priorities dominate strategy.

Nevertheless, a perfectly splendid tourist trip awaits the history buff who travels from Elkton, Maryland, where the British landed, to the Battle of Brandywine battlefield, up the Great Valley to Immaculata University where the Battle of the Clouds took place, over to the Battlefield of the Paoli Massacre, crossing the Schuylkill and going to Whitemarsh, then to Fort Washington, and back up Bethlehem Pike to Germantown Avenue, and down to the Chew Mansion. The campaign for the conquest of Philadelphia ended with the fall of Ft. Mifflin, when the British fleet was finally able to re-supply Howe's army. This direct auto tour is a little out of chronological sequence, but it can be done in one day if you don't dawdle. If you slow down and spend an extra day, you can include the Moland House where Washington waited to see where General Howe was going. At the right season, there's hawk watching on the ridge at Fort Washington Park, and maybe on to Trenton, or even up the New Jersey waist to Perth Amboy on lower New York Bay, where the Howe brothers began and ended their Philadelphia adventure. That would take you past Princeton and New Brunswick, or even include a trip to the Monmouth Battleground. With this extension, you have traveled much of the extent of the Revolutionary War in the Mid-Atlantic states.

http://www.philadelphia-reflections.com/blog/2109.htm

Modern Printing and Post-Modern Printing

There are many more authors than publishers of books. Since almost every school child owns and uses a home computer, this disparity might be even greater except for a technical barrier between home computers and high-speed printing presses in the way they treat illustrations. A presently insurmountable mismatch arose from commercial printing presses migrating from movable type (i.e. Gutenberg style) to page-images, whereas the computer industry aimed for cheap printers which perfected the Gutenberg method instead of replacing it.

Modern Print Press

Commercial printers need to produce high volume output inexpensively, while cheap computer printers produce low-volume output and disregard a rather high unit price. Most of the barriers between the two have been overcome, except for photos and other detailed images. Let's give a simplified explanation.

Since 1993 when Adobe invented the method, commercial printers generally work from what amounts to a photograph of each page, called a PDF or "portable description format". To some extent, portions of a page can be stitched together like a patchwork quilt, but of course all the pieces must be uniform in their technology. The industry standard is that everything is printed at 300 dots per inch. That's essentially 300 pixels per inch. The establishment of this standard made it possible for huge high-speed presses to produce hundreds of pages of newsprint a minute on machines which cost millions of dollars apiece. Commercial printing during the first half of the Twentieth century accepted the massive cost of the printing machine in order to promote production speed. Home computer printers sacrificed production speed in order to become cheap. Profitability comes from the ink, not the printer.

Low-volume desktop printers can afford to take the time to examine each character or image as it comes along and readjusts appropriately. Essentially, computer printers do individual typesetting every time a new page is printed. They are thus able to exploit considerable compression for storage, or for the speed of electronic transmission for printing at a remote location. For them, 72 dots per inch are sufficient, since computer- driven printers have acquired the facility to guess the gaps between dots (dithering) well enough to fool the eye of the reader. Since the same thing is true of display monitors, there is resistance in the computer industry to sacrificing the interests of the multitude to the needs of those comparatively few authors and publishers who use the mass-printing industry to keep their unit costs low. Computer printing squashes thousands of pixels down to 72 per inch.

But it's hard to convert photo images back from 72 to 300 dpi since the dithering trick won't stretch that far. A good illustration is the washing of wool socks. You can throw argyle socks in a washing machine and they will shrink to the size of baby booties, but they won't stretch back up if you decide to wear them. The usual expedient is to enlarge a small picture and take a second picture of it, then enlarge the enlargement, and so on. Alternatively, the Genuine Fractals program by Altamira Group comes closer to achieving the desired result, but even it has limits.

When someone has more than a very few pictures that need stretching between Internet screen display and commercial printers, the current best advice is to store two different-density copies of the same image, and use as required.

Print Press

Slight re-design of work flow is advised to create still a third version of the image, for the purpose of storage. The biggest possible image with the most pixels possible should be stored on the author or publisher's own computer. A second, shriveled 72-dpi, image is sent to be stored on the host computer of a website, and can be used for desktop printing as well. When commercial printing happens to be desired, the much larger stored image can be shriveled to 300 dpi by conversion of a page to PDF format, or else (for editing) this third version of the image is incorporated into Office Word, subsequently re-incorporated back into a pdf file for final printing. PDF conversion is quick and simple once a decision is made as to what the final product should look like after it is printed.

Fine art display or other highly demanding graphics will follow this general outline, as well. Those who have any aspiration for high-density output would be well advised to go back to the original photograph. In 2008, that translates into another maxim for the photographer who takes the original picture: Always take all photos in RAW format, with a view toward later flexibility of use. Less demanding output can be produced from degraded copies of the RAW original, the most common of which is now the so-called JPEG format. Those who discard an original RAW image, are almost always sorry. And those who buy cheaper cameras that go straight to JPEG are just asking for frustration. Now that memory chips have become cheap, the extra technology to generate the RAW image does not greatly increase the cost of a camera, but greatly enhances its ability to retouch images without breaking up in the repeated dithering and re-dithering usually required for retouching. A number of steps in the photography process could be eliminated if the user would accept the requirement of some new step resembling retouching as part of every snapshot.

http://www.philadelphia-reflections.com/blog/1530.htm

Sylphs in Passing

It requires only one brief tour of any large Art Museum to become convinced the world's definition of feminine beauty has passed through many styles. Obesity of Titian proportions seems to be making a come-back at the moment, so being slender might not persist as the standard of feminine beauty indefinitely. However, at the present moment slender seems to have it. It has been claimed with authority the average woman is fifteen pounds overweight, so that became the basis for the old English weight measure of a stone, fourteen pounds. Some fierce feminists have even legitimized this factoid as an invention of domineering men. Establishing ideal weight as one stone less than average weight would fiendishly condemn woman-hood to eternal torture by hunger trying to achieve ideal proportions, achievable perhaps but seldom achieved. If so, the two chief fiends would turn out to be William Shakespeare and Alexander Pope, who are chiefly responsible for at least a poetic glorification of that slender woman, the sylph.

We return a little closer to the world of the probable when we notice that girls are typically a little too thin before the age of reproduction, and a little too heavy after the menopause, almost disregarding race, ethnicity, religion, or changing fashions in beauty. Physical activity and muscle tone have something to do with this age-related phenomenon, adding issues of pot bellies and poor posture to the aging mix. In any event, it's fairly factual that the average woman really is about one stone heavier than the current standard, for whatever reason and of course with notable exceptions.

Philadelphia Sylphs

It also happens that sick women, especially those affected with cancer, lose weight effortlessly. Their outgrown clothes, usually the expensive pieces, have been saved in a closet for that promised day when they can summon the grit to lose fifteen pounds. And sadly, when illness approaches, they do. For a few months the flash of returning beauty can be quite striking.

The doctors of their acquaintance notice it first, and for the most part do not comment aloud about it. A quick sober glance toward a doctor friend silently confirms the opinion, while each soberly recognizes yet another example of being sorry to get what you wished for. A few even know the famous aphorism of the father of the specialty of Neurology, Silas Weir Mitchell: "Those who have not known sick women, do not know women."

http://www.philadelphia-reflections.com/blog/2158.htm

Brave New World

Let me put some emphasis on what I consider the most revolutionary change of a current lifetime. Nothing to do with Hitler, Stalin or Mao; or jet planes, television and computers. Or even the rise of the impoverished underdeveloped world. To me, the most revolutionary change of the past century has been the extension of the average life span, by thirty or forty extra years, depending on where you happen to live. I'm proud to be a member of the profession at the center of it.

Jobless

Right in the middle of this revolution, the Great Depression of the Thirties convinced a great many people there were not enough jobs to go around. The Union movement, as we say, or the Socialist movement as they come right out and call it in Europe, adopted a general thesis that a limited number of jobs should be shared equally so everyone could have a chance at them. Child labor should be condemned, and those occupying "decent" jobs should retire early. A number of lesser agitations of the Thirties have the same sound to them: piecework was a bad thing because it encouraged women to work at home, depressing prevailing wages. Home offices might be condemned by the IRS for similar reasons. Automation and efficiency generally were resisted. Since I persist in the notion that efficiency is almost always a very good thing, these anti-efficiency campaigns sound like more hidden agendas to spread the supposedly limited amount of available work. General thesis: if there are not enough high wage jobs for everybody, low-wage jobs still remain an evil thing. Indolence is better. In the redistributionist world, no proposal has any merit if it leads to accepting lower wages, even temporarily.

While some oppose efficiency, few want to live shorter lives. Even victims of self- inflicted conditions generally draw back when consequences become fully visible. Mistaking a lifetime of paychecks for a lifetime of work, they wish to extend one without extending the other. That's usually called inflation, and it seldom creates wealth, so part of the idea is to lower expectations for everybody. It's vaguely possible that alcoholism, unsafe sex and recreational drug consumption are efforts in that direction, but more likely those confused souls are just that, confused.

That's where matters seemed to rest until recently. People didn't specifically ask for this extra longevity, and while willing to risk it, are not willing to lose it. My own elderly generation can start to see signs that a protracted retirement can eventually lead to running out of money, so there is a need for experimentation and innovation about making retirement a more productive period of life.

Great Depression of the Thirties

And then I heard some college kids talking; kids do talk a lot. The proposition argued was essentially as follows: Instead of adding a few years to your retirement, when you are feeble and useless, why not deliberately offer kids an extended period of loafing, when health is good, love-making is vigorous, and endurance of the debilitating effects of recreation is strong? A grungy lifestyle is more tolerable for someone who is thirty, than for the same person at seventy-seven, so it could be an overall cheaper lifetime. An additional five years of pizza for breakfast; sounds heavenly.

Boys and girls react to this proposal in biologically different ways, of course. Boys don't have the same biological clock, telling them they better start their families while they still can. Raising little children is strenuous, particularly in time shared with continuing education, starting a career, or finding a husband. Getting a divorce is also a surprisingly debilitating distraction, seldom recommended by those who have experienced it. The males have an easier time loafing; so why not return to the customs of a century ago, when girls planned to get married during the same summer they graduated from college. Because part of that tradition was "Don't get married until your ship comes in," it tended to define an eligible male as someone thirty years old. Unfortunately, that interferes with another new trend, the buddy system.

Most girls now expect to go to college, and colleges have mostly become coeducational to accomodate the market. Hand in hand kids stroll the lawns of academe, more like siblings than lovers. The faculty marvels at this phenomenon, which to them seems like an unfamiliar mixture of incest and promiscuity, but it does not quite follow the rules of either entertainment. Since it is surely related to the increasing divorce rate, universally condemned as a bad thing, the buddy system may yet evolve into something else. It's been suggested men should get over their traditional reluctance to raise someone else's children. Now there is an idea, that is going to take some time to get used to. It's in a class with willingness to continue employment at age eighty-five, just so someone else can wander around without shaving, at age twenty-five.

So, all in all, we ought to swallow our generational pride and just do what our grandparents did. Men should wait until thirty to get married, while women should marry at twenty; simple. It forces feminists to admit that in some sense they are inferior to men, so declare victory and call it an innate superiority of women. It also calls the pseudo- sibling pairings of school children into question, which is essentially the only thing new in this whole business. It's probably a lot of fun, but it exacts too high a social price.

http://www.philadelphia-reflections.com/blog/2159.htm

Is Stock Trading Passe?

Moore's Law is named after Gordon Moore, who pointed out that computer chips seemed to double their speed every few years, an important issue affecting the cost of computers and the heat they give off while operating, and so on. In fifty years, there have been enough doublings of speed to make it often irrelevant whether they get any faster for the job they are intended

Gordon Moore

to do. No one really cares whether a blink of an eye gets any quicker. The question is beginning to arise whether it makes any practical difference if the trading of stocks gets faster.

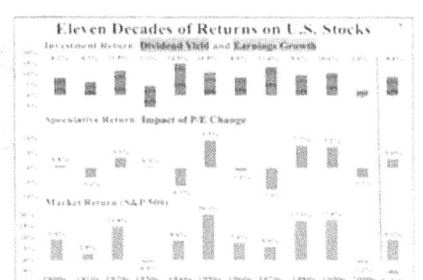
Returns on U.S. Stocks

At the moment, it's widely quoted that 70% of stock trades on major exchanges are now conducted between two unattended computers; it won't be long before 100% are. All of the inefficiencies of trading pits, with shouting and shoving, winking and maybe some front- running, will vanish into the humming of progressively smaller electric machines. Kinks will appear then get ironed out, perhaps after another Long Term Capital episode or two. The cost of trading will become vanishingly small, essentially a chess game between mathematics wizards. But volatility will smooth out, and costs will become negligible. So far as we can see, that's the end of the line, beyond which a computer speed sixteen times as fast serves no extra purpose.

John Bogle

But John Bogle, who invented the index fund and grew Vanguard to several trillions in assets, amused himself recently in front of a bedazzled audience. Several large funds, maybe even a lot of them, are taking what looks like a static mass of sleeping stocks and trading them internally at a rate of thousands per second, hoping to make a tiny fraction of a penny per trade individually, and a whole lot of profit for the managers in aggregate, while giving the appearance of standing still. Is this a good thing or a bad thing? Hard to say. John Bogle seems to imply it might even be a bad thing. Whatever it is, it is not the end of the line.

For completeness, look at the opposite end of this spectrum. Once more, it is John Bogle who points out that the price of stock can be divided into its earnings, its dividends, and its speculative volatility. Total earnings for the past century have averaged 9.1%, but if you strip off the effect of price-to-earnings variance, you have an investment return of 8.8%, essentially the same in the eyes of normal people. The way an investor could strip away the P/E volatility – is to buy the whole company. When you own the whole company, public opinion stops influencing the price. Holding companies can do that, as can private equity funds, and even Warren Buffett. If you are playing this game, all you need is a big-enough holding company with honest management, or at least one independent method for estimating a fair price. If you are a value investor like Warren, buying the company for a P/E ratio well below 12.5 and holding it forever, you ought to achieve a return which significantly exceeds 8.8%. If you are an investment bank on Wall Street, you may buy the stock cheap, fix it up, and sell it rather soon for a much higher P/E ratio. Either way, there are transaction costs and taxes only twice, when you buy it and when you sell it. An investment company can do all kinds of things, but an individual investor should know enough to adjust his buying (of shares of these intermediaries) to a youthful stage of life, and his selling to his retirement years. It cannot be claimed the quirks have been completely worked out, but it's a start. Come back in a few years and see what has been added to this idea to make it air-tight.

http://www.philadelphia-reflections.com/blog/2177.htm

Medical Generation Gap

To understand the dynamics of the following medical anecdote, the reader should understand the thrust of Miriam's First Rule of Management. Miriam is my oldest daughter, with long experience managing many firms, large and small. Her rule is that when an employee starts misbehaving for no good reason, eliminate the position. Invariably, well almost invariably, an employee who starts acting out doesn't have enough work to do. If you are managing a large organization, you should also consider firing the supervisor of that person, on the grounds the supervisor should have noticed there was not enough work for the employee to do, and is probably covering up.

Miriam Schaefer

My anecdote concerns a session at the 2006 annual meeting of the American College of Physicians, ostensibly devoted to conflict between generations of doctors. It didn't take long before the meeting turned into an uproar about the new work rules which prohibit a resident physician from working more than 80 hours a week. That's supposed to protect patients against mistakes of sleepy doctors, although some suspect it is mainly an outgrowth of a gap between what they do and what they expected to do. From the time they entered high school, future doctors have been taught to expect workaholic employment conditions, and while more normal people haven't been taught that message, that's irrelevant. The situation is aggravated by the increased admission of women to the profession, who for their part have been taught to expect a breathless race between finishing their work and getting home to relieve the baby-sitter. Perhaps in time the newly invented specialty of "hospitalists" will get established and accepted, along with accident room work as another harrowing occupation which abruptly ends its day by the clock rather than the backlogs. At the moment the pioneers must overcome the suspicion, only partly fair, that Miriam's First Rule applies to them.

"Medical care certainly ain't what it used to be!"

If not, that Rule clearly does apply to the youngsters who now must go home to spend quality time with their families, because they are not allowed to exceed the new work rules. At the ACP meeting, a dozen of us Civil War veterans were treated to an appalling amount of teenage mumbo jumbo apparently emanating from unsuspected warfare between Generation X and the Baby Boomers, their supervisors, mentors, and colleagues. All of us Civil War veterans held the private opinion that Baby Boomers were a little self-indulgent, but in the eyes of Gen Xers the boomers are workaholic fanatics, incapable of relaxing even for a moment in order to enjoy the life of the good, the true and the beautiful.

As we passed out of the room at the end of the session, one of the silent gentlemen with white hair came over to me. We didn't know each other, but we recognized the signs of a silent shared opinion. The old doctor leaned over to me and muttered, "They offer nothing, but they want everything." I smiled, and we parted. I guess I might have told him about Miriam's First Rule, but it would have taken too much explaining.

http://www.philadelphia-reflections.com/blog/823.htm

Taxes as a Form of Consumption

About half of the American public pays federal income taxes, and among the half who don't, a great many receive a green government payment check, meaning they have negative income taxes. The tax assistance companies, H. and R. Block and the like, had little for their offices and staff to do in January, February and March until someone hit on the idea of processing "fundable tax credits" for a fee. That is, the lower-income segments of the population get the promise of an April tax "rebate" as the consequence of tax-form preparation, so H. and R. Block just loans them the money, discounted for fees and interest. It keeps staff busy, generates revenue. Hardly anyone in the upper income half of the population is aware of all this, so

Refund Check

there is little political friction. This whole system of income redistribution quite effectively keeps the two halves of the population sitting in the same chairs at the tax-preparation offices, but in different months of the year; one half getting paid, the other half coughing up the payments.

Tea Tax

It thus becomes possible for two inflammatory slogans to bandy about, without starting fistfights or revolutions. The first was overheard at a local bank, one stranger remarking to another, "Has it ever occurred to you that taxes are a form of consumption?" To which the other person replies, "Yes, and taxes are the largest expenditure I make." A nation which once went to war over a two-cent tax on tea is remarkably passive about the ways things have evolved, but this essay is not devoted to unfairness. Prepare to hear how the upper income brackets might reduce their taxes, whether that counts as decreased consumption or not. Whenever you tax something, you get less of it; if you tax public income more, the public will earn less. So, this little essay is serious when it proposes that we all earn less, so we can get taxed less. And being taxed less, we need save less for our retirements.

The general principle is this: income is usually taxed in the year it is earned, with some exceptions, rebates and deferrals. The exceptional situations are often referred to as "loopholes" and therefore live in political jeopardy. However, if a person spends

Taxation

the money or dies while these deferrals continue to exist, the income may escape taxation entirely. In a sense, the largest loophole of all lies in the present fact that nearly half the population pays no income taxes at all, so saving income earned under those circumstances may lead to investment capital, which is later spent during highly taxed periods of that same person's life.

Money earned by a child, usually on investments donated by a relative, is an example. Since at present, a child may receive annual gifts of $13,000 tax-free, as much as a half-million dollars can be accumulated in this way, always at the risk that laws may be changed and, further, at risk of spendthrift abuse by a psychopathic child. Whether these are wise risks for a parent to take, depends in large part on what sacrifices are made for the purpose, especially loss of parental restraint of unwise spending. A much more serious argument grows out of the possibility that money in the hands of children who lack experience in deferred gratification may actually provoke recreational drug use, or other sociopathic behavior.

Finally, lack of planning may create opportunities as much as planning does. A person who has paid little attention to financial planning may arrive at an advanced stage where life expectancy is considerably shorter. Savings at that point may be divided into money on which deferred taxes must be paid when you spend it, and money on which taxes have already been paid. More savings will be consumed if the individual triggers deferred tax liabilities, than if he just uses up money on which taxes have already been paid. Therefore, if he ignores lifetime habits and spends after-tax capital first – the whole nest egg will last longer. But none of this deferred-income tax issue can compare with the problem of income on which taxation has been completely forgiven at the time it was spent, the so-called tax expenditures. The largest such tax expenditures are on the interest of home mortgages, on employer-paid (but not self-paid) health insurance, and employer- paid retirement income. Of these, the least consequential are the retirement income, because the tax is merely deferred, not completely forgiven. The two biggest items are home mortgages, which lie at the root of the 2007 financial crash, and employer-paid health insurance premiums, which triggered the Obama health proposal of 2009. The Obama plan purports to rein in health costs, but is estimated by the Congressional Budget Office to cost the Treasury $100 billion a year.

Extra! In the Fall of 2011, this boring matter suddenly came to the surface, in the form of huge American deficits threatening to bankrupt the country, as they were apparently actually going to do in Greece. As politicians do, many attempts were first made to rename the over-spending issue for partisan advantage. It was, for instance, tax expenditure. It was, possibly, a sovereign debt crisis. In any event, the Congressional Budget Office included such wealth redistribution under the heading of **tax expenditure**, which totaled a trillion dollars. Since everyone was searching for a painless category to eliminate in order to balance the budget, this term was hard to avoid. As far as Congress is concerned, the national deficit is whatever the CBO says it is, and in this case it lumped a lot of things together which politicians would like to split apart. When you take things in small pieces, it becomes possible to boil the frog by slowly heating it up before it realizes it is cooked. Lumping things together induces the frog to jump out of the pot, but however that may be, it has got lumped together by the referee of such matters, and there is a strong possibility it will stay lumped.

The essential point for accountants to focus on, is that tax expenditures are all counted as revenue when any non-accountant can see they are expenses. For political speech-making purposes, this distinction is vital and no opponent will let another politician wiggle out of it. And the beauty part of it is that it also spotlights three of the most besetting evils of modern politics: the tax exclusion of employer-based health insurance, the home mortgage interest tax exclusion, and the "earned" income tax credit. The first of these is responsible for our health insurance mess, and the other is responsible for our home mortgage crisis; the two main political problems of the day are suddenly plopped into the limelight, just when a lot of people are looking for ways to hide them. Furthermore, this bombshell was fired by a panel of the four outstanding tax economists of the nation, each of them roundly denouncing them as unthinkable ideas that never should have been born in the first place. Alan Greenspan, famous for unintelligible speech, simply said all of these tax expenditures, every one of them, should be eliminated immediately. One would hope that is clear enough. Martin Goldstein, formerly chairman of President Reagan's Council of Economic Advisors, agreed. As did former Governor Engler of Michigan, widely acknowledged to have rescued his state from impending bankruptcy. Senator Nelson, a Democrat from Florida and chairman of the committee, positively beamed with pleasure. It was hard to think this was anything but a turning point in history; let some political candidate disagree, and he can expect to have his audience shown a videotape of this succinct epic in the history of Senatorial hearings. These greybeards said, in what was obviously an unrehearsed moment, just eliminate these three terrible ideas in one stroke, and the national deficit will be reduced by a trillion. That's what they said, and it's easily proved that they had said it.

http://www.philadelphia-reflections.com/blog/2129.htm

State in Schuylkill Fishing Club

Richard Romm, a rising historical scholar with a special interest in early Philadelphia, recently educated the Right Angle Club in the history of the Schuylkill Fishing Club in the State in Schuylkill, and was immediately accepted into membership. Of the Right Angle, that is, which is an old club by some standards, but scarcely a hundred years old in the eyes of the really old, old clubs.

Richard Romm

The State in Schuylkill is an eating club, originally a fishing and eating club, apparently organized around the annual shad run up the river. The clubhouse, or Castle, was moved several times, in response to damming of the river, and is now located on the grounds of, or adjoining the edge of, Nicholas Biddle's estate on the Delaware River called Andalusia. One by one, the Atlantic Ocean rivers of America have been dammed and their annual shad migrations brought to an end, except through the city of Richmond, Va, so there was little point in moving The Castle to follow the fish. It remains overlooking the Delaware in spite of its name.

Andalusia

There seem to have been several name changes, the most important of which was to change the Colony of Schuylkill to State of Schuylkill for obvious reasons. Originally, the Castle was roughly opposite the falls of Fairmount on the West Bank of the Schuylkill at about Girard Avenue; thus, from 1732 to 1822 located on Baron Warner's property called Eaglesfield. In 1822 it moved to Rambo's Rock (the Rambo family is said to be the oldest European settler family in Pennsylvania) opposite Bartram's Gardens, then finally in 1887 to Andalusia, Nicholas Biddle's country estate. The club was founded in 1732, and dates of movings are possibly hazy, possibly somewhat because of the reluctance of club officers to return the calls of inquiring historians. The State in Schuylkill claims to be the oldest organized men's club in the world, an honor contested by White's in London. The roots of this argument are found tangled in the vital issue of whether their age should be based on the formal organization of the clubs, or on the establishment of the coffee houses which housed the original clubs. Four books are said to have been written about club history, but we depend here on Mr. Romm.

There is an unclear relationship with Chief Tammenend, possibly traceable to the shad run. May 1 is St. Tammany's day, growing into the fancy that he was the "Patron Saint of America", before a branch of the nation-wide association opened in New York and sort of tarnished up the name. Other traditions of the club have to do with wearing Mandarin hats, possibly having to do with the export of gensing which was once abundant in our colonial suburbs, with a return cargo of Chinese dishware. All of the cooking is done by official citizens of the club. The quantities of food are remarkable; one 19th Century menu listed eleven pounds of meat per member. The club drink is a punch, the famous Fishhouse Punch, widely recognized to be rather strong. Its inventor is reputed to be Edward Shippen Willing, on the occasion of the first visit to the clubhouse by women guests. The quantity of alcoholic beverage at these events is especially remarkable in view of the Quaker origins of many original members of the club, but not necessarily of the guests. Among the various guests were Generals Grant, Meade and McClellan. Dinner begins with two traditional toasts: to George Washington, and to Captain Sam Morris. Washington was appropriate enough, having a history of drinking a bottle of Madeira every day at lunch. But Sam? Captain Sam the Quaker?

Free Quaker Meetinghouse, Fifth and Arch Streets

Somewhere in this tradition are allusions to the Free Quakers, Quakers who abandoned the peace testimony to fight the British. There is also the tradition of hostility to British rule which antedates the Revolution, and may have some connection to the fanciful contention that their little state was not really part of Penn's colony. Captain (of the City Troop) Sam was a stalwart, possibly the sole founder, of the Gloucester (N.J.) Fox-hunting club. The history is passed down that 22 of the original 26 members of the First City Troop were members of the fox- hunting club, and many if not most were Quakers. The first "Governor" of the State in Schuylkill was Thomas Stretch, but the second Governor, from 1766 until his death, was Captain Sam. He was repeatedly referred to as the life of the club, and held in the highest esteem by all. He was "read out" of the main Quaker Meeting, not so much for his drinking as for his flouting of Quaker belief in pacifism. He reputedly led a sabre charge at the Battle of Trenton, and was a leader of the City Troop in that revolution within a revolution at James Wilson's house, which rescued at least four future signers of the Constitution from a mob of militia which momentarily turned Jacobin.

Naturally, descendants of Quakers on both side of this uproar have been reluctant to say much about it. But somewhere within the history of Samuel Morris must be some important clues about the 18th Century splits within the Quaker Church, to say nothing of the revolt of the three Quaker colonies against British rule.

http://www.philadelphia-reflections.com/blog/2192.htm

Nanoparticles: The Dwarfs are Coming

Professor Shyamelendu Bose of Drexel University recently addressed the Right Angle Club of Philadelphia about the astounding changes which take place when particles are made small enough, a new scientific field called nanotechnology. In one sense, the word "nano" comes from the Latin and Greek for "dwarf". In a modern scientific sense, the nano prefix indicates a billionth of something, as in a nanometer, which is a billionth of a meter. Or nanotubes, or nanocalcium, or nano anything you please. Nanometer is likely to be the dominant reference, because it is around this width that particles begin to act strangely.

Professor Shyamelendu Bose

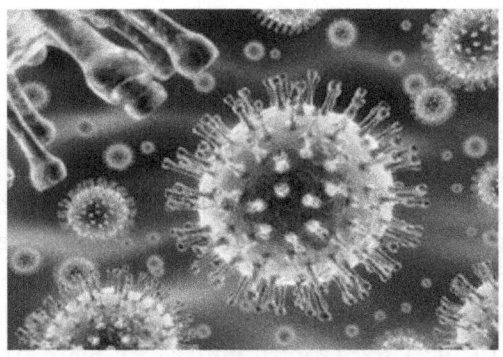

Nanoparticles

At this width, normally opaque copper particles become transparent, cloth becomes stain-resistant, and bacteria begin to emit clothing odor. Because the retina is peculiarly sensitive to this wave length, colors assume an unusual brilliance, as in the colors of a peacock's tail. Stable aluminum powder becomes combustible. Normally insoluble substances such as gold become soluble at this size, malleable metals become tough and dent-proof, and straight particles assume a curved shape. Damascus steel is unusually strong because of the induction of nanotubes of nanometer width, and the brilliance of ancient stain-glass colors is apparently created by repeated grinding of the colored particles.

Practical exploitation of these properties has almost instantly transformed older technologies, and suggests the underlying explanation for others. International trade in materials made with nanotechnology has grown from a few billion dollars a year to $2.6 trillion in a decade, particularly through remaking common articles of clothing which were easily bent or soiled, into those which are stain and water resistant. Scientists with an interest in computer chips almost immediately seized upon the idea, since many more transistors can be packed together in more powerful arrangements. Richard Feynman of Cal Tech seems to be acknowledged as the main leader of this whole astounding field, which promises to devise new methods of drug delivery to disease sites through rolling metal nanosheets into nanotubes, then filling

Richard Feyman of Cal Tech

the tubes with drug for delivery to formerly unreachable sites. Or making nanowires into various shapes for the creation of nanoprostheses.

Cal Tech on Los Angeles

And on, and on. At the moment, the limitations of this field are the limitations only of imagination about what to do with it. For some reason, carbon is unusually subject to modification by nanotechnology. It brings to mind that the whole field of "organic" chemistry is based on the uniqueness's of the carbon atom, suggesting the two properties are the same or closely related. For a city with such a concentration of the chemical industry as Philadelphia has, it is especially exciting to contemplate the possibilities. And heartening to see Drexel take the lead in it. There has long been a concern that Drexel's emphasis on helping poor boys rise in the social scale has diverted its attention from helping the surrounding neighborhoods exploit the practical advances of science. The impact of Cal Tech on Los Angeles, or M.I.T on Boston, Carnegie Mellon on Pittsburgh, and the science triangle of Durham on North Carolina seems absent or attenuated in Philadelphia. We once let the whole computer industry get away from us by our lawyers diverting us into the patent-infringement industry, and that sad story has a hundred other parallels in Philadelphia industrial history. Let's see Drexel go for the gold cup in this one – forget about basketball, please.

http://www.philadelphia-reflections.com/blog/2193.htm

A Change of Era

Amaxim of the book-editor trade is "Deviate from chronology at your peril." Two events may have little to do with each other, but it always remains possible to show the earlier event had somehow affected the later one. An editor may know little about a topic, but he knows that much.

In 2011, I was privileged to be a tuition-paying student at one of Yale's Directed Studies Courses. An invention of former Dean Donald Kagan, the DS courses take an important era in history and apply three conventional faculty disciplines to it at once: Philosophy, History and Literature. For the undergraduates, courses range in chronology from Ancient Greek to the Enlightenment; so far, the alumni just get the Greeks. Judging only from the course in Ancient Greek, the unspoken thesis soon emerged that a major era experiences permanent changes in history, philosophy and literature, but the connection between the three is often loose, requiring some pondering to make the connections firm.

Dean Donald Kagan

Aeschylus does have connection with Plato, and Aristotle with Thucydides but it remains unclear why the connection exists. Furthermore, you can lump these things or split them; Ancient Greece fits naturally with the Roman Empire, but it can also stand alone. Therefore, although the Yale faculty tends to lump the American Revolution with The Enlightenment, a consideration of the life and times of Robert Morris, Jr. fits naturally with both the Enlightenment and the American Era, because the American part of the Enlightenment bifurcates abruptly when Morris stood in debate with William Findlay in the Pennsylvania State House in 1798 – and lost.

Robert Morris

Morris was the richest man in America or close to it, the unofficial President of the United States in its darkest hours, the most brilliant non-academic innovator in Western Finance, the leader of American high society, the only man beside Roger Sherman to sign the Declaration of Independence, the Articles of Confederation, and the Constitution. Morris did not realize it but he was within a few months of going to jail for three years, then spending his final five years in secluded disgrace. Robert Morris was not accustomed to losing arguments, but he lost this one, concerning the wisdom of continuing the charter of the Bank of North America, the first real bank of the country. He lost an argument he should have won easily. In retrospect, the new modern American Era was beginning, and he was apparently on the wrong side of it. Politically, that is. Speaking purely of banking and finance, he was a century ahead of his time.

It seemed to me and my alumni classmates that the idea of examining an historical period in the light of three different academic disciplines, gradually assumed considerable merit. The philosophy department examines beliefs which underlay action, and the history department describes what those actions turned out to mean inhuman affairs. But the literature department comes far closer than either of the other two, to imparting to a reader just what it was like to be an ancient Greek. Professor Kagan seems to have a really good idea here, although it must be resource-expensive to develop, academically. Three departments of Academia have to come to some sort of agreement about the whole synthesis, an agreement which surely must not have been present at the start. It must be a process highly similar

Ancient Greek Gods

to a medical school teaching about a disease, with coordinated input from pathologists, surgeons and internists. A nice idea, but terribly labor-intensive of labor of the highest quality. Book editors would say it is safer to stick with chronology as an organizing principle, if you plan to do a lot of organizing. Nevertheless, I must express my gratitude to Yale for allowing me to be a spectator at an experiment conducted by masters of the thinking trade. Its results can only be judged by standards other than the usual ones.

http://www.philadelphia- reflections.com/blog/2179.htm